The Works of George W. Cable

Arlin Turner

EDITOR

Old Creole Days (New York, 1879)
The Grandissimes (New York, 1880)
Madame Delphine (New York, 1881)
The Creoles of Louisiana (New York, 1884)
Dr. Sevier (Boston, 1885)
The Silent South (New York, 1885)
Bonaventure (New York, 1888)
Strange True Stories of Louisiana (New York, 1889)
The Negro Question (New York, 1890)
John March, Southerner (New York, 1894)
Strong Hearts (New York, 1899)
The Cavalier (New York, 1901)
Bylow Hill (New York, 1902)
Kincaid's Battery (New York, 1908)
"Posson Jone" and Père Raphael (New York, 1909)
Gideon's Band, A Tale of the Mississippi (New York, 1914)
The Amateur Garden (New York, 1914)
The Flower of the Chapdelaines (New York, 1918)
Lovers of Louisiana (New York, 1918)

MR. GEORGE W. CABLE

Reproduced from *The Critic,* XXXIV (March,1899), 204.

STRONG HEARTS

BY

George W. Cable

With an Introduction and Notes by

ARLIN TURNER

GARRETT PRESS, INC.

New York, 1970

SBN 512-00075-1
Library of Congress Catalog Card
Number 77-96495

The text of this book is a photographic reprint of the first edition,
published in New York by Charles Scribner's Sons in 1899.
Reproduced from a copy in the Garrett Press Collection.

First Garrett Press Edition Published 1970

Manufactured in the United States of America

GARRETT PRESS, INC.
Publishers
250 West 54th Street, New York, N.Y. 10019

INTRODUCTION

George W. Cable discovered Creole New Orleans for literature. In works extending from his first story in 1873 to his last novel in 1918, he gave his native city a full and discriminating embodiment such as perhaps no other American city has received in the writings of a literary figure. Although some of his works are set outside the city, particularly in outlying regions of Louisiana and Mississippi, his best and most characteristic fiction portrays the French and the American civilizations in their struggle, from the Louisiana Purchase onward, for dominance in New Orleans. He lived the first forty years of his life in the city and knew it from both observation and study. He was old enough to register impressions ten years before the Civil War, and through lively traditions in the family his memory seemed to extend back farther. A questioning observer of events around him and an eager student of local history, he stored up the materials which later entered his stories and novels. To an extent that holds for only a few, if any, of our other novelists, Cable's major works deal with the issues confronting his region in his time and derive in important ways from his own experiences and observations.

Cable was born in New Orleans on October 12, 1844, to parents who had migrated from Indiana after the panic of 1837. His father, George Washington Cable, was a native of Virginia; his mother, Rebecca Boardman, was of New England descent. They owned slaves and seem to have adjusted comfortably to life about them, while remaining aware that theirs was the most European of all American cities. The father died in 1859, leaving his widow and four children all but penniless. The son George dropped out of school and began work without finishing high school.

After the fall of New Orleans to the Union forces, an event that Cable witnessed at the levee and in the streets and afterward recounted in both historical and fictional works, he joined the Confederate cavalry on October 9, 1863. Only five feet two inches in height and weighing no more than a hundred pounds, he was wounded twice but stood up to the demands of the desperate campaigns in Mississippi and Alabama until the surrender. He was mustered out in May, 1865.

As a clerk and bookkeeper, he continued the reading and study he had done even as a soldier. In December, 1869, he was married to Louise Stewart Bartlett. The next year he became a reporter for a New Orleans daily, the *Picayune*, and for a year and a half also provided a column of miscellaneous comment entitled "Drop Shot," first weekly and later daily. His writings were still sought for the *Picayune* after he had returned to work in business, and he furnished occasional feature articles and editorials. He welcomed especially an invitation to write editorials in a futile war the *Picayune* waged in 1872 against the Louisiana Lottery Company. His interest in local history sent him to archival records and early newspapers to gather information for a series of newspaper articles published under the title "The Churches and Charities of New Orleans."

These inclinations toward history and toward social criticism and reforms were reflected in the stories that Cable, in 1873, began publishing in *Scribner's Monthly Magazine*. Since he thought of the present as an extension of the past, stories of earlier time were to his mind suitable vehicles for comment on current affairs. After collecting seven magazine stories in the volume *Old Creole Days* (1879), he wrote his first novel, *The Grandissimes* (1880), pleased to have the greater scope of the novel for the portrait of the Creole civilization he had already begun drawing and for the criticism he wanted to level at current society. He was also hopeful that the novel would yield the income he must have before he could cut his business ties and give full time to writing. In 1881 appeared the novelette *Madame Delphine,* and in 1884 the novel *Dr. Sevier* and a historical work, *The Creoles of Louisiana.*

Readers of these five books, all published in a span of five years, were introduced to the Vieux Carré, the ancient square that had been laid out when Bienville founded New Orleans in 1718. In Cable's time the old square was still occupied mainly by Creoles, proud descendants of French and Spanish colonials, and as much as possible remained separate from the American city across Canal Street upriver. With interests already pricked by Bret Harte and others who had written about the people and manners and terrain of distant regions, readers were fascinated by the characters and the life they encountered on Cable's pages. Reviewers found the word "charm" all but essential in commenting on the stories. Nathaniel Hawthorne's sister Elizabeth, in a fragment preserved at the Huntington Library, mentioned "Jean-ah Poquelin" to her niece, the novelist's daughter Una, presumably soon after the story was printed in *Scribner's Monthly* in May, 1875. It is "a tale that struck me," she wrote; "it is original and impressive, and lingers in my mind. It is a story of the early days of American rule in Louisiana. I forget the author's name, but whoever he is, he has genius, and a field for its exercise, among the mixed races and strange manners of the South West."

Cable recognized the literary ore everywhere around him, waiting to be mined. It was his habit to make notes on the spot as he encountered likely materials—to record a descriptive detail, a dialectal phrase, the words of a *patois* song, or its tune. He had an acute ear for speech and could write down the musical scores of songs he heard on the street. He tended in his early fiction to introduce excessive detail from history and observation—such at least was the opinion of his editors, who were more concerned than he was with the conventional elements of plot. Similarly, his pursuit of accuracy caused him to burden his early stories with something close to literal transcription of dialect—chiefly the English of his French-speaking characters at various levels of education and acquaintance with the language, but including also the dialect speech of Spanish, Italian, German, and Irish characters. Satisfactory methods of representing dialect in fiction—indeed the legitimacy of dialect in literature at all—had not yet been determined. With experience, and prompted by protests against his dialect from readers and editors, Cable evolved a method which would drop any attempt at full delineation in favor of bare suggestion, mainly by occasional locutions, pronunciations, or simple foreign phrases. In applying the new method, he revised *The Grandissimes* for a new edition in 1883 by simplifying the Creole dialect. The charm of his stories continued nevertheless to owe much to the dialect speech of his characters. Howells and Twain and Cable's friends among his publishers liked to insert dialect expressions in their letters to him or to declare that they talked nothing but Creole.

The stories of *Old Creole Days* recognizably belong to the same unique locality; but for all they have in common in setting, theme, and technique, there are wide variations among them, suggesting an inclination in the author toward experiment with materials, effects, and means. At one extreme in tone and emotional response is "Madame Délicieuse," the story of a young woman who employs her beauty and her talents to conquer both a lover and his father, a stubborn Creole of an older, unbending genera-

tion. The laughter of Creole women on the balconies along
Royal Street in the old city, the fragrance of orange
blossoms which meets the wedding party emerging from
the church—such are the ingredients which produce the
charm of the story. At the other extreme is "Jean-ah
Poquelin," set at a mysterious, ancient dwelling on the
bank of an overgrown drainage canal at the edge of the
swamp. Stubborn Creole independence, antagonism to all
encroachments of government and society, whispered
rumors of slave-smuggling, fratricide, and even greater
transgressions give way finally to the actualities of leprosy,
death, and unsuspected self-sacrifice.

" 'Tite Poulette" delineates in low key but with great
force the quadroon women of New Orleans: quiet,
resigned victims of a social system they have no hope of
escaping. The escape of 'Tite Poulette, because it can be
proved that she is white, the daughter of Spanish
immigrants, makes the doom of the quadroons the more
inexorable. Over against the delicacy, the hinting, and the
indirection of this story may be set the broad comedy, the
gargantuan feats of strength performed in "Posson Jone' "
by the intoxicated parson from the remote parishes, and
the equally extravagant contrasting portrait of Jules St.
Ange, a young Creole who is adept in all the ways to get
along in the city. A different contrast, no less pronounced,
is furnished by "Café des Exilés," in which intrigue,
stealth, betrayal, and death are enacted through the
confused intermingling of refugees from the Caribbean
Islands engaged in gun-smuggling.

The stories of *Old Creole Days* portray the strange and
the picturesque; and these elements, stressed by the local
colorists, have some prominence in most of Cable's other
fiction. Even his earliest stories, however, defy classifica-
tion simply as local color fiction. For one thing, Cable
often added touches of stern realism, although his

materials might seem to belong to romance, and although he might throw over them the haze of remote indefiniteness. His inclination, as a matter of fact, was to admit unpleasantness of concept and language and to present qualities of human character and action not as a rule present in the American fiction of his time. All his works before 1900 were published first in magazines, and the editors often urged revision to make them acceptable in "family" magazines. Even so, much of their distinctive flavor remained. For another thing, Cable drew characters of a greater variety, with subtler qualities of mind and spirit and greater psychological realism than was usual with the local colorists. The title character in his first published story, " 'Sieur George," and Injun Charlie in the second story, "Belles Demoiselles Plantation," might be cited, and also the title character in "Jean-ah Poquelin." Moreover, the voice of social criticism is clear in several of the stories. The result is that, even in this early work, Cable brings his special region into real existence, while drawing characters who suggest the vitality and depth to be achieved in longer works, and while adding threads of social comment which give his fiction a direct relationship to its time and place.

As Cable read Louisiana history, its chief fact after 1803 was the political, commercial, and cultural rivalry of the Creoles and the intruding *Américains*. This rivalry echoes in the stories "Jean-ah Poquelin" and "Madame Délicieuse"; and it provides the structure of *The Grandissimes,* which was planned as a dramatization of the clash between the two civilizations.

Cable undertook to display in *The Grandissimes* the full sweep of peoples and forces in New Orleans in the first years after the Louisiana Purchase, when the Creoles were by no means ready to transfer their allegiance from the French Emperor to the American President, or the President's representative, Governor Claibourne. The multitudinous Grandissime family and the others within their sphere include one who accepts the new political and social order, another who allows no quarter to the forces of change, a young Creole widow and her daughter (whom Howells placed among his favorite characters of fiction), and others who represent the compact, interwoven Creole society.

Some of the Creoles objected that Cable chose too large a proportion of his Creole characters from the lower classes, and that the dialect speech he gave them was not accurate. Other Creoles testified in the New Orleans newspapers that they found his characters and their speech true to life. Cable often declared that he was fond of the Creoles, and he obviously admired much in their character, but he also found faults to condemn. The displeasure of the Creoles was in part, perhaps, what might be expected of any distinctive people who found themselves introduced into fiction—even if the writer was one of their own number, and surely if he was an outsider. Still, Cable could not conceal—did not try to conceal—his impatience with the Creoles' clannishness, with their lack of concern for social betterment, and with what to his mind was their lax morality. As a consequence, a Creole already critical of American encroachment on his Gallic culture could not help resenting books in which he was portrayed—rather than simply praised—by an American for other Americans.

Whatever resentment the Creoles felt on this account was inflamed when they found in *The Grandissimes* views on the race question which were anathema to them. Soon after the Civil War, Cable saw that the former slaves were often denied basic citizen's rights. As a newspaper reporter he had seen the folly of segregated schools, and in 1875 he wrote a letter on the matter to a New Orleans newspaper. But a rejoinder by the editor printed along with his letter and his failure to get a second letter published in any newspaper reminded him that his views were at odds with those held by his friends and business associates. He avoided the topic for the next ten years, except for indirect statements in his fiction, as in "Belles Demoiselles Plantation" and " 'Tite Poulette." The first story he had submitted in 1872, "Bibi," was rejected by several editors, mainly because of what it implied in picturing the tragic fate of a proud African prince in slavery. The story remained unpublished until it was incorporated in *The Grandissimes* as the episode of Bras Coupé. This novel, with its tone set by the elemental story of Bras Coupé, presents several victims of racial oppression: Clemence, the ancient purveyor of voodoo charms, who is shot in the back, in a sort of lynch killing, after she has been told to run for her life; the beautiful quadroon Palmyre, who hopelessly loves the white Honoré and scorns the love of Honoré Grandissime, f.m.c. (free man of color), who drowns himself because of his disappointment in love as well as in other areas which are controlled by the fact that he is not white. The white Honoré defies the taboos of his clan—and of the South at large—by entering into business partnership with his f.m.c. half-brother and thus pointing toward a future, the author implies, when the errors and the injustices of race would be left behind. The author speaks at times as author, and the character Frowenfeld has something of an authorial role as intermediary among the characters and as judge of all that takes place; even so, the social comment comes across to the readers mainly through situation and action. The reader is drawn into the life being portrayed and feels the forces bearing on the characters.

The Grandissimes succeeds in its purpose of recreating an era in the history of New Orleans. It delineates the social strata from the apex of the dominant race to the slaves newly brought from Africa, and activities from a parade of government officials to the making of a voodoo charm. The complicated plot reflects the complex inter-relations among individuals, families, and classes in the confused era represented. Though the action is set in a distant historical past and clarity is handicapped at times by indirection and indefiniteness and the play of conceal-ment and revelation in the narration, there is a firm sense of actuality, created in part by the density of the life portrayed.

In 1881 Cable published the novelette *Madame Delphine,* which he said in the preface to a new edition in 1896 was written because a quadroon had charged him with falsifying the story of 'Tite Poulette. In this story he would tell the truth: the beautiful daughter is indeed a quadroon, but her mother swears a lie so that she can marry the white man she loves. When the mother has confessed the lie and has died in the confessional, the priest mutters, "Lord, lay not this sin to her charge!" Perhaps in no other work did Cable achieve such balance and mutual reinforcement of character, scene, and event, supported by such a consistent tone as in *Madame Delphine.*

Cable was glad to write *The Creoles of Louisiana* (1884), he said, to show his affection for the Creoles and dispel any belief that he had treated them unkindly in his fiction. He had first written, in connection with the Tenth Census of the United States, a work entitled *History and Present Condition of New Orleans* (1881). Afterward he adapted it for serial publication in the *Century Magazine,* January-July, 1883, with illustrations by Joseph Pennell, which were reproduced in the book. The materials of this history are of a type to invite a historian, or a novelist; the romance of the exploration and early settlement, the ravages of the cholera, yellow fever, and flood from the river, the vicissitudes of political ties—to France, Spain,

France again, the United States, the Confederacy, and the Union afterward. Here Cable had occasion to move extensively in the area he had already explored in his fiction. A comparison of the three published versions shows him successively reducing the proportion of bald facts in his account and approaching the methods of fiction.

Cable's second novel, *Dr. Sevier,* is set in New Orleans but is not a Creole story. It has only one Creole character, Narcisse, an auxiliary character who serves also to provide comedy in a story that is otherwise dark. In contrast to *The Grandissimes,* this novel has only three characters of any prominence, Dr. Sevier and a young couple, the Richlings, and the plot is simple. As first planned, this was to be a story of prison reform. Cable was at the time immersed in a campaign to reform the New Orleans prisons and asylums, but as composition progressed, this thread was superseded by an exploration of the themes of poverty, charity, work, pride, and the human relations which revolve about them. The New Orleans setting is all but ignored. Inundation and yellow fever are introduced, to be sure, but only as normal elements in the scene. It is likely that Cable wanted to show that he could write fiction which was not dependent on the Creoles and the romance of early New Orleans. But it seems more likely that the plot he conceived required ordinary people, such as the Richlings, who would face ordinary events in commonplace situations, and yet would suffer pain, ignominy, and tragedy which are no less severe for the unexcited way in which they present themselves. Cable had read Howells' *A Modern Instance* early in the composition of *Dr. Sevier* and undertook to employ Howellsian realism in presenting through different characters differing views of subjects he wanted to explore.

With the publication of *Dr. Sevier* in 1884, Cable was

established, at home and abroad, on the level of William Dean Howells, Henry James, and Mark Twain. Indeed, it was not uncommon for him to be ranked above one or more of them. He was often compared with Nathaniel Hawthorne and with the major French novelists of the nineteenth century—without suffering in the comparison. He continued to publish for another thirty-four years, but his literary output never afterward equaled the rate or, with possibly one or two exceptions, the quality of his early work. His literary production fell off after 1884 because his platform readings from his works and his reform work absorbed so much of his time and energy.

Soon after leaving his accountant's desk late in 1881, Cable knew that his literary work would not furnish the income he needed. By the end of 1883 he was popular in the North and East as a platform reader. During four months of 1884-1885 he traveled with Mark Twain on a joint tour, which set the high mark in an era when many authors gave public readings. These readings provided a major part of his income for another twenty years. He shared the platform on occasion with James Whitcomb Riley, Hamlin Garland, and Eugene Field. In 1898 and again in 1905, he went to England for a reading tour.

In the summer of 1884 Cable moved his family to Simsbury, Connecticut, to be near his publishers and the main lecture circuit. A year later he settled permanently in Northampton, Massachusetts, where Smith College, he said, offered an attraction for a man with six daughters. A son had died of yellow fever in 1878 in New Orleans; another son died in 1908 at the age of twenty-three. Besides his own family, Cable furnished varying degrees of support for his mother, his unmarried sister Mary Louise, his widowed sister Antoinette Cox, and her two children, all of whom moved to Northampton.

Cable was never long without a part in some reform

effort. From work in his church in New Orleans for social betterment, he moved on to organize a widely acclaimed program for reform of the New Orleans prisons and asylums. Next he studied the penitentiary reports from the twelve Southern states which leased convicts to labor for private contractors, and wrote an attack on the system which he delivered before the National Conference of Charities and Correction and published afterward in the *Century Magazine,* February, 1884, with the title "The Convict Lease System in the Southern States." His study of prison records had convinced him that former slaves received a special kind of justice in the courts. Under the title "The Freedman's Case in Equity," he opened the subject, first in an address before the American Social Science Association and afterward in the *Century Magazine* for January, 1885. The essay provoked intense opposition throughout the South, with the most persistent and virulent attacks printed by the New Orleans newspaper the *Times-Democrat,* which earlier had sponsored Cable's campaign for prison reform. The Creoles too now raised shrill voices in the outcry.

Cable was confident that once the subject was discussed openly, reasonable solutions could be reached. He visited the South regularly, to freshen his memory for the benefit of his fiction, he said, and to keep aware of developments. By writing, speaking, organizing others to debate the issues, and distributing his own and other pertinent writings, he undertook to speak for what he called "The Silent South" in the title of one of his essays—meaning the majority of Southerners who he thought held his views but were voiceless while the politicians and the journalists spoke in tones of reaction. A volume of his essays, *The Silent South,* appeared late in 1885; a second edition, with supplements, in 1889; and another volume, *The Negro Question*, in 1890. The essays in these books present the most inclusive, the most carefully reasoned argument yet published for extending full civil rights to the Negroes. His appeal was to reason, fairness, morality, and justice. Reducing the entire problem to a question of right and wrong, and therefore a problem having but one answer, he could make no room for expediency or gradualism. Thus he championed public education, universal suffrage, an end to segregation, and every assistance to help the freedman rise above the handicaps of slavery and deprivation.

Reluctantly and sadly, Cable realized by 1890 that there were no avenues for him to continue his efforts. The Southern states, with general approval in the North, were establishing legal barriers intended to keep the Negroes in a segregated, nonvoting status. The public platform was effectually closed to discussion of the great sore question, as he called it, and even his editors at the *Century Magazine* now rejected his polemical essays. He still had no doubt as to the ultimate outcome, and he wrote a prediction in his notes that the rise of the Negro race after emancipation would be "the great romance of American history."

In 1894 Cable published *John March, Southerner,* a novel in which he traced out with great care the bewildering intricacy of the Southern problem, and indicated not an exact program, but the direction in which he believed steps must be taken. The writing of the novel had been slow and painful, partly because he was embodying opinions only then being sifted out in his mind, and partly because he struggled—without success—to make the novel acceptable to the editor of the *Century,* Richard Watson Gilder, who wanted no further treatment of the Southern question, in fiction or otherwise. (The novel was finally serialized not in the *Century,* but in *Scribner's Magazine* and was published as a book by Charles Scribner.) Simply by introducing into *John March*

the complex Southern mind, the tensions between classes
and castes and sections, the tradition of the frontier, with
its components of danger, heroism, and violence, the cult
of chivalry—by drawing into his plot the full scope of the
Southern character and experience following the Civil War,
Cable moved a long way toward the modern Southern
novel. He portrayed in realistic detail the post-Reconstruc-
tion South: the growth of industry, outside capital and
outside management, development—or exploitation—of
natural resources, public works, new stresses on schools
and churches, political corruption, betrayal by Southern
leaders. As in *Dr. Sevier* ten years earlier, various
characters express in action and speech varied opinions on
the issues.

John March progresses through misconception, error,
and wrongheadedness. He has more humanity—more
failings and aberrations—than Frowenfeld in *The Grandissimes*, or Honoré Grandissime. Like Dr. Sevier, he has
abundant human contradictions. He comes to understand
himself and to understand his region in the same process,
for as the title indicates, he and the South are identical.
Many aspects of his career and his outlook parallel the
author's. His decision, finally, to decline the inviting
opportunities outside the region and to dedicate his energy
and talents to the future of the South may be taken to
mean that Cable in some degree regretted moving north; at
least it shows that he believed his move had lessened the
effectiveness of his work for reform in the South.

Even before Cable realized that campaigning for Southern reform was no longer feasible, he had begun a program
for social betterment in Northampton. He had begun in
1887 the reading clubs which evolved into the Home
Culture Clubs, later the People's Institute, which remains
active today. Another endeavor of his was the Northampton Prize Flower Garden Competition, which prompted

one who had observed the competition several years to publish an article with the title "How One Man Made His Town Bloom." Cable's study of theories of gardening and his experience in the Northampton program resulted in a series of magazine essays and a book, *The Amateur Garden* (1914). His church work reached an apex in the Bible class he taught in the City Hall, which particularly invited non-church-goers and reached an attendance of 700 men.

Early in his career as an author, Cable planned to write about the Cajuns, descendants of the Acadians expelled from Nova Scotia in 1755 who had settled on the prairies and along the bayous of Southwest Louisiana. He had traveled in the Cajun country and had made warm friends there. Three magazine stories about the Cajuns were combined into *Bonaventure* (1888), though there is little to unify them except a few characters continued from one story to another and the simple life of the isolated communities. The stories presented a region and a people all but unknown to literature, but the homely, even primitive, virtues and faults of the characters, and their resignation to deprivation contrast sharply with the qualities which had proved so attractive in his Creole characters.

Three other separate stories were joined to make a volume, *Strong Hearts* (1899). Although set in or near New Orleans, these stories make little attempt to exploit the region or any of its particular inhabitants. Instead, they stress character delineation. The best of the three, "Gregory's Island," is a convincingly realistic study of a man who isolates himself on a remote island, with no means of escape for a predetermined period of battling against his thirst for drink. The novelette *Bylow Hill* (1902) is unique among Cable's works. It is set not in the South but in New England, though it has characters from the South, and it owes nothing to characters or events of the author's own observation. It is a study of abnormal psychology, in which a gifted young minister is destroyed by an irrational, blind jealousy of his wife. Although there is little in this work to suggest Cable's other fiction, the narrative method is well adapted to the plot, and the minister comes across as a believable character.

Beginning with *The Cavalier* (1900), Cable settled into a pattern which continued the rest of his life: writing slowly, with frequent interruptions occasioned by other demands on his time, drawing advances from his publisher to meet his expenses, and beginning a new novel before its predecessor was off the press. Thus were produced *The Cavalier* and three more novels: *Kincaid's Battery* (1908); *Gideon's Band* (1914); and *Lovers of Louisiana* (1918). He began still another novel, to be set in New Orleans at the time of World War I, but did not finish it.

In his later years Cable wintered in the South as a rule, but otherwise continued his routine and his community activities at Northampton. His first wife died in 1904. He married Eva C. Stevenson in 1906; and after her death in 1923, he married Mrs. Hanna Cowing. He died at St. Petersburg, Florida, January 31, 1925, and was buried at Northampton.

Cable's late novels are well made. They show a masterful handling of dramatic scene, dialogue, climax, and suspense. They draw heavily on the author's knowledge of Louisiana and the river, and especially his experiences as a soldier. These novels are what the author intended: romances of love and war or some other source of excitement and suspense, and they are skillfully managed. But instead of the sense of actuality which prevails in *The Grandissimes, Dr. Sevier,* and *John March,* his characters are idealized and their problems are neither profound nor moving.

The Cavalier had a larger immediate sale than any other book Cable wrote; and a dramatized version was successful on the stage. "The author did not have to read up to write this story," reads an inscription Cable wrote in a copy of the book. The narrator within the plot, Richard Thorndyke Smith, who had appeared earlier in stories and essays as an authorial spokesman, has experiences closely following Cable's war experiences. But everything is recalled over the haze of years. Nothing is said of the issues behind the war, or of the soldier's day-to-day experience of boredom, fear, and suffering. Cable had returned from that war thirty-five years earlier; he had returned from his individual campaign for Southern reform more recently and had turned from that defeat to write idealized romances instead of realistic novels of social criticism. He had kept up the struggle for reform more than a dozen years; reformers do not often exceed that term.

Kincaid's Battery is another romance of the war, with the artillery replacing the cavalry of *The Cavalier* and with the action centered around New Orleans instead of Northern Mississippi. Again the military action, the confusion and excitement of battle, reflects the author's familiarity with his materials, though his recollection is blurred by time and a deliberate idealization.

Cable called *Gideon's Band* a romance—and rightly. His plan was to recreate the steamboat traffic his father had known on the Mississippi River in the 1840's and 1850's. But the book suggests that Cable could no longer ignore the problems he had debated in his early works. Perhaps he realized that his treatment of those problems had given his early stories and novels the immediacy, actuality, and moral ballast which provided their strength. In the character Phyllis, the lot of the quadroons is again dramatized, but with only negative answers offered: the solution for Phyllis is not in flight to the North or in marriage to a white man. In the main plot, Cable returned to a theme repeated in his early work, both fictional and historical: the erosion of character which often resulted from the social dominance enjoyed by the aristocratic whites of the South, their wealth and pride, and especially their station above both poor whites and blacks.

In *The Flower of the Chapdelaines,* formed from three earlier stories and published in March, 1918, Cable returned to Creole characters and Creole speech and still more pointedly to the Southern questions he had argued more than thirty years earlier. In all three stories, which belong to slave times, and in the enveloping framework, which has its own love plot, Cable's views on the race question are implied rather than asserted. His last novel, *Lovers of Louisiana,* published later in the same year, opens all the old questions again. One member of the Durel family, Zéphire, has Creole narrowness and family pride in extravagant measure, but is repudiated by his father and by his sister Rosalie, who possesses the beauty and charm of Cable's earlier Creole women and has also an understanding of public affairs that would have been inappropriate to the earlier women. Her marriage to Philip Castleton represents a joining of the best from the Creole and the American civilizations and prophesies a better future for the South. Philip Castleton has much in common with John March, and he is identical with the author in much of what he does and what he thinks. He decides to remain in the South, hoping to help usher in the peace and justice so long absent. The character Ovid Landry, a Negro engaged in business with the Durel family, to the profit of all concerned, was modeled on a bookseller Cable knew while visiting New Orleans to gather materials for the book. *Lovers of Louisiana* is a novel of social criticism, Cable's first since *John March, Southerner* twenty-four years earlier. The presence of social comment, reflecting both conviction and feeling in the author, gives the novel some of the strength and interest of the early fiction.

The two threads of Cable's career—as social critic and reformer and as fiction writer—were fused in his best works and otherwise remained close and parallel. His "Drop Shot" newspaper column ran heavily to social comment and led him to begin writing stories. By the time his first stories were published in 1873, he realized that the former slaves were being denied the rights of citizenship, and he was convinced that, as had been true under slavery, both races would suffer as a consequence. But for another dozen years he confined his direct efforts for reform to areas such as prisons and asylums where he would have wide public approval. He dared broach the matter of Negro rights only indirectly in his fiction, especially in *The Grandissimes, Madame Delphine,* and several stories. His case for social reform gained strength from the force of these works and in turn furnished them with weight and immediacy they otherwise would have lacked.

When Cable launched his open campaign for greater Negro rights in 1884, he pushed his literary work to the back of his desk and published no extended work until *John March, Southerner,* ten years later. Although this novel has no equal in its detailed presentation and analysis of the Southern scene in the decade after Reconstruction, it is a successful work of fiction. It displays convincing realism of scene and character and a perceptive delineation of the relations present in a community during a transition period which demands radical changes in institutions and attitudes. Here, as in the early works, the social reformer and the novelist became one, and the reformer's zeal was an asset to the novelist.

With the Southern debate closed soon after 1890, Cable's reforming zeal found an outlet in the reading clubs and the flower garden competition. With publishers unreceptive to novels with the unpleasantness and the controversial social comment of *The Grandissimes* or *John March*, Cable turned to the historical romance. In a series of essays, he justified the romance not as a work that would convey the experience of real characters in real situations, whether current or historical, facing important social and moral problems—as he would have characterized *The Grandissimes;* rather, he justified the romance as a form of fiction that would "make you feel to-day that you are entertained, and find to-morrow that you are profited." Cable's books after 1900 conform to this pattern (though the last, *Lovers of Louisiana*, shows him less satisfied with it).

In only five of the forty-five years in Cable's literary career he produced most of his best work. Of his later writings, some belong with his best; most of them show great care in planning and execution and all but flawless management of the narration; and some of them contain memorable scenes or characters. But in his first five books Cable staked off a literary claim, Creole New Orleans, which no one has seriously challenged. He delineated the Creole and the American civilizations, confronting each other for more than a century, in a composite portrait in which each accentuates the qualities of the other; he reproduced the speech and songs of the region with a skill that Mark Twain declared had no equal; he portrayed a gallery of characters remarkable for their variety and their vividness; and running through his works is a firm, perceptive social commentary which normally augments the literary effectiveness.

The Plan of This Edition

The nineteen volumes in the Collected Edition of George W. Cable in the American Authors Series includes all his major writings. Only two of the works he published separately have been excluded: *The Busy Man's Bible* (Meadville, Pa., 1889), composed from periodical articles on the study and teaching of the Bible; and *A Memory of Roswell Smith* (privately printed, 1892), a tribute to his publisher friend. Cable brought most of his magazine writings together in volumes of stories and essays, all of which are printed in the Collected Edition. The writings from his pen which do not appear in this edition include the contents of his "Drop Shot" column in the New Orleans *Picayune*, 1870-1872; miscellaneous uncollected sketches and essays in periodicals; a completed short story, an unfinished novel, and other fragments he left in manuscript; notebooks he kept at intervals, particularly during his visits to England in 1898 and 1905; and letters.

All volumes in the Collected Edition of Cable are reproductions of the first editions. For *The Silent South*, the appendix which Cable added in the 1889 edition is reproduced here from that edition. The preface in the 1896 edition of *Madame Delphine* is printed as an appendix in this edition.

Arlin Turner
Duke University

Selected Bibliography

Books

Biklé, Lucy L. C., *George W. Cable: His Life and Letters* (New York: Charles Scribner's Sons, 1928).

Butcher, Philip, *George W. Cable: The Northampton Years* (New York: Columbia University Press, 1959).

_____, *George W. Cable* (New York: Twayne Publishers, 1962).

Cardwell, Guy A., *Twins of Genius* (East Lansing: Michigan State University Press, 1953).

Dennis, Mary Cable, *The Tail of the Comet* (New York: E. P. Dutton, 1937).

Ekström, Kjell, *George Washington Cable: A Study of His Early Life and Work* (Upsala: Lundequistska Bokhandeln; Cambridge, Mass.: Harvard University Press, 1950).

Rubin, Louis D., Jr., *George W. Cable: The Life and Times of a Southern Heretic* (New York: Pegasus, 1969).

Turner, Arlin, *George W. Cable: A Biography* (Durham, N.C.: Duke University Press, 1956).

_____ , *Mark Twain and George W. Cable: The Record of a Literary Friendship* (East Lansing: Michigan State University Press, 1960).

_____, *George W. Cable* (Austin, Tex.: Steck-Vaughn Company, 1969; Southern Writers Series).

Articles

Bartlett, Rose, "How One Man Made His Town Bloom," *Ladies' Home Journal,* XXVII (March, 1910), 36, 80, 82.

Baskervill, William M., *Southern Writers* (Nashville, Tenn., 1897-1903, 2 vols.), I, 299-356.

Bentzon, Th. [Marie Therèse Blanc], *Les Nouveaux Romanciers Américains* (Paris, 1885), pp. 159-226.

Butcher, Philip, "George W. Cable and Booker T. Washington," *Journal of Negro Education,* XVII (Fall, 1948), 462-68.

_____ , "George W. Cable and Negro Education," *Journal of Negro History,* XXXIV (April, 1949), 119-34.

Eidson, John Olin, "George W. Cable's Philosophy of Progress," *Southwest Review*, XXI (Jan., 1936), 211-16.

Ekström, Kjell, "The Cable-Howells Correspondence," *Studia Neophilologica,* XXII (1950), 48-61.

Hearn, Lafcadio, "The Scenes of Cable's Romances," *Century Magazine,* XXVII (Nov., 1883), 40-47.

Howells, W. D., *Heroines of Fiction* (New York, 1901, 2 vols.), II, 234-44.

Hubbell, Jay B., *The South in American Literature* (Durham, N.C., 1954), pp. 804-22.

Lorch, Fred W., "Cable and His Reading Tour with Mark Twain in 1884-1885," *American Literature,* XXIII (Jan., 1952), 471-86.

Manes, Isabel Cable, "George W. Cable, Fighter for Progress in the South," in *A Southerner Looks at Negro Discrimination: Selected Writings of George W. Cable* (New York, 1946), pp. 11-18.

Pattee, F. L., *A History of American Literature Since 1870* (New York, 1915), pp. 246-53.

Toulmin, Harry Aubrey, *Social Historians* (Boston, 1911), pp. 35-56.

Turner, Arlin, "George W. Cable's Revolt Against Literary Sectionalism," *Tulane Studies in English,* V (1955), 5-27.

_____, "George W. Cable's Beginnings as a Reformer," *Journal of Southern History,* XVII (May, 1951), 135-61.

_____, "George Washington Cable's Literary Apprenticeship," *Louisiana Historical Quarterly,* XXIV (Jan., 1941), 168-86.

_____, "A Novelist Discovers a Novelist: The Correspondence of H. H. Boyesen and George W. Cable," *Western Humanities Review,* V (Autumn, 1951), 343-72.

Wilson, Edmund, *Patriotic Gore* (New York, 1962), pp. 548-87, 593-604.

Textual Note

The first edition of *Strong Hearts,* which is reproduced here, was published by Charles Scribner's Sons on March 11, 1899. It was bound in green sateen cloth, and the pages were trimmed to 7 inches by 4¾ inches. See Jacob Blanck, *A Bibliography of American Literature,* II (New Haven, 1957), 8.

The three stories comprising this book had been published in *Scribner's Magazine* as follows: "The Solitary" (entitled "Gregory's Island"), XX (August, 1896), 149-59; "The Taxidermist," XIII (May, 1893), 679-88; and "The Entomologist," XXV (January-March, 1899), 50-60, 220-27, 315-26.

Strong Hearts

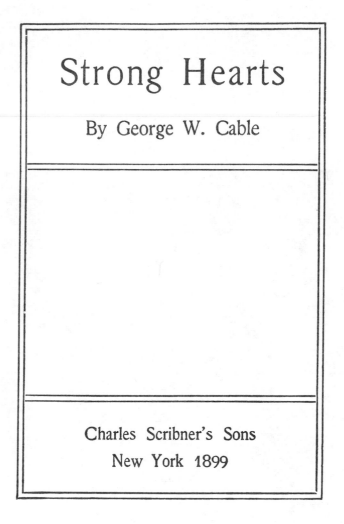

Strong Hearts

By George W. Cable

Charles Scribner's Sons
New York 1899

TROW DIRECTORY
PRINTING AND BOOKBINDING COMPANY
NEW YORK

CONTENTS

$*^*_*$ *In magazine form " The Solitary" appeared under the title
of " Gregory's Island."*

The Solitary

The Solitary

I

" THE dream of Pharaoh is one. The seven kine are seven years; and the seven good ears are seven years: the dream is one. . . . And for that the dream was doubled unto Pharaoh twice, it is because the thing is established." . . .

In other words: Behind three or four subtitles and changes of time, scene, characters, this tale of strong hearts is one. And for that the tale is tripled or quadrupled unto you three or four times (the number will depend); it is because in each of its three or four aspects—or separate stories, if you insist—it sets forth, in heroic natures and poetic fates, a principle which seems to me so universal that I think Joseph would say of it also, as he said to the sovereign of Egypt, " The thing is established of God."

3

Strong Hearts

I know no better way to state this principle, being a man, not of letters, but of commerce (and finance), than to say—what I fear I never should have learned had I not known the men and women I here tell of—that religion without poetry is as dead a thing as poetry without religion. In our practical use of them, I mean; their infusion into all our doing and being. As dry as a mummy, great Joseph would say.

Shall I be more explicit? Taking that great factor of life which men, with countless lights, shades, narrownesses and breadths of meaning, call Religion, and taking it in the largest sense we can give it; in like manner taking Poetry in the largest sense possible; this cluster of tales is one, because from each of its parts, with no argument but the souls and fates they tell of, it illustrates the indivisible twinship of Poetry and Religion; a oneness of office and of culmination, which, as they reach their highest plane, merges them into identity. Is that any clearer? You see I am no scientist or philosopher, and I do not

4

The Solitary

stand at any dizzy height, even in my regular business of banking and insurance, except now and then when my colleagues of the clearing-house or board want something drawn up—" Whereas, the inscrutable wisdom of Providence has taken from among us "—something like that.

I tell the stories as I saw them occur. I tell them for your entertainment; the truth they taught me you may do what you please with. It was exemplified in some of these men and women by their failure to incarnate it. Others, through the stained glass of their imperfect humanity, showed it forth alive and alight in their own souls and bodies. One there was who never dreamed he was a bright example of anything, in a world which, you shall find him saying, God—or somebody—whoever is responsible for civilization—had made only too good and complex and big for him. We may hold that to make life a perfect, triumphant poem we must keep in beautiful, untyrannous subordination every impulse of mere self-provision, whether earthly or heavenly, while at the same time we give life

5

its equatorial circumference. I know that he so believed. Yet, under no better conscious motive than an impulse of pure self-preservation, finding his spiritual breadth and stature too small for half the practical demands of such large theories, he humbly set to work to narrow down the circumference of his life to limits within which he might hope to turn *some* of its daily issues into good poetry. This is the main reason why I tell of him first, and why the parts of my story—or the stories—do not fall into chronological order. I break that order with impunity, and adopt that which I believe to be best in the interest of Poetry and themselves. Only do not think hard if I get more interested in the story, or stories, than in the interpretation thereof.

The Solitary

II

THE man of whom I am speaking was a tallish, slim young fellow, shaped well enough, though a trifle limp for a Louisianian in the Mississippi (Confederate) cavalry. Some camp wag had fastened on him the nickname of " Crackedfiddle." Our acquaintance began more than a year before Lee's surrender; but Gregory came out of the war without any startling record, and the main thing I tell of him occurred some years later.

I never saw him under arms or in uniform. I met him first at the house of a planter, where I was making the most of a flesh-wound, and was, myself, in uniform simply because I hadn't any other clothes. There were pretty girls in the house, and as his friends and fellow-visitors—except me—wore the gilt bars of commissioned rank on their gray collars, and he, as a private, had done nothing glorious, his appearance was always in civilian's dress. Black he wore, from head to foot, in the cut fashionable in New Orleans when the war brought fashion to a stand: coat-waist high, skirt solemnly long; sleeves and trousers small at the hands and feet, and puffed out —phew! in the middle. The whole scheme was dandyish, dashing, zou-zou; and when he appeared in it, dark, good-looking, loose, languorous, slow to smile and slower to speak, it was—confusing.

One sunset hour as I sat alone on the planter's veranda immersed in a romance, I noticed, too late to offer any serviceable warning, this impressive black suit and its ungenerously nicknamed contents coming in at the gate unprotected. Dogs, in the South, in those times, were not the caressed and harmless creatures now so common. A Mississippi planter's watch-dogs were kept for their vigilant and ferocious hostility to the negro of the quarters and to all strangers. One of these, a powerful, notorious, bloodthirsty brute, long-bodied, deer-legged —you may possibly know that big breed the planters called the "cur-dog" and prized so highly—darted out of hiding and silently sprang at the visitor's throat.

8

The Solitary

Gregory swerved, and the brute's fangs, whirling by his face, closed in the sleeve and rent it from shoulder to elbow. At the same time another, one of the old "beardog" breed, was coming as fast as the light block and chain he had to drag would allow him. Gregory neither spoke, nor moved to attack or retreat. At my outcry the dogs slunk away, and he asked me, diffidently, for a thing which was very precious in those days—pins.

But he was quickly surrounded by pitying eyes and emotional voices, and was coaxed into the house, where the young ladies took his coat away to mend it. While he waited for it in my room I spoke of the terror so many brave men had of these fierce home-guards. I knew one such beast that was sired of a wolf. He heard me with downcast eyes, at first with evident pleasure, but very soon quite gravely.

"They can afford to fear dogs," he replied, "when they've got no other fear." And when I would have it that he had shown a stout heart he smiled ruefully.

9

Strong Hearts

"I do everything through weakness," he soliloquized, and, taking my book, opened it as if to dismiss our theme. But I bade him turn to the preface, where—heavily scored by the same feminine hand which had written on the blank leaf opposite, "Richard Thorndyke Smith, from C. O." —we read something like this:

The seed of heroism is in all of us. Else we should not forever relish, as we do, stories of peril, temptation, and exploit. Their true zest is no mere ticklement of our curiosity or wonder, but comradeship with souls that have courage in danger, faithfulness under trial, or magnanimity in triumph or defeat. We have, moreover, it went on to say, a care for human excellence *in general,* by reason of which we want not alone our son, or cousin, or sister, but *man everywhere,* the norm, *man,* to be strong, sweet, and true; and reading stories of such, we feel this wish rebound upon us as duty sweetened by a new hope, and have a new yearning for its fulfilment in ourselves.

"In short," said I, closing the book, "those imaginative victories of soul over

circumstance become essentially ours by
sympathy and emulation, don't they?"

"O yes," he sighed, and added an indis-
tinct word about "spasms of virtue." But
I claimed a special charm and use for unexpected and detached heroisms, be they fact·
or fiction. "If adventitious virtue," I argued, "can spring up from unsuspected
seed and without the big roots of character——"

"You think," interrupted Gregory,
"there's a fresh chance for me."

"For all the common run of us!" I cried.
"Why not? And even if there isn't, hasn't
it a beauty and a value? Isn't a rose a rose,
on the bush or off? Gold is gold wherever
you find it, and the veriest spasm of true
virtue, coined into action, is true virtue, and
counts. It may not work my nature's
whole redemption, but it works that way,
and is just so much solid help toward the
whole world's uplift." I was young enough
then to talk in that manner, and he actually
took comfort in my words, confessing that
it had been his way to count a good act
which was not in character with its doer

as something like a dead loss to everybody.

"I'm glad it's not," he said, "for I reckon my ruling motive is always fear."

"Was it fear this evening?" I asked.

"Yes," he replied, "it was. It was fear of a coward's name, and a sort of abject horror of being one."

"Too big a coward inside," I laughed, "to be a big stout coward outside," and he assented.

"Smith," he said, and paused long, "if I were a hard drinker and should try to quit, it wouldn't be courage that would carry me through, but fear; quaking fear of a drunkard's life and a drunkard's death."

I was about to rejoin that the danger was already at his door, but he read the warning accusation in my eye.

"I'm afraid so," he responded. "I had a strange experience once," he presently added, as if reminded of it by what we had last said. "I took a prisoner."

"By the overwhelming power of fear?" I inquired.

"Partly, yes. I saw him before he saw

me and I felt that if I didn't take him he'd either take me or shoot me, so I covered him and he surrendered. We were in an old pine clearing grown up with oak bushes."

"Would it have been less strange," I inquired, "if you had been in an old oak clearing grown up with pine bushes?"

"No, he'd have got away just the same."

"What! you didn't bring him in?"

"Only part of the way. Then he broke and ran."

"And you had to shoot him?"

"No, I didn't even shoot at him. I couldn't, Smith; *he looked so much like me.* It was like seeing my own ghost. All the time I had him something kept saying to me, 'You're your own prisoner—you're your own prisoner.' And—do you know? —that thing comes back to me now every time I get into the least sort of a tight place!"

"I wish it would come to me," I responded. A slave girl brought his coat and our talk remained unfinished until five years after the war.

III

GREGORY had been brought up on the shore of Mississippi Sound, a beautiful region fruitful mainly in apathy of character. He was a skilled lover of sail-boats. When we all got back to New Orleans, paroled, and cast about for a living in the various channels " open to gentlemen," he, largely, I think, owing to his timid notion of his worth, went into the rough business of owning and sailing a small, handsome schooner in the " Lake trade," which, you know, includes Mississippi Sound. I married, and for some time he liked much to come and see us—on rainy evenings, when he knew we should be alone. He was in love yet, as he had been when we were fellow-absentees from camp, and with the same girl. But his passion had never presumed to hope, and the girl was of too true a sort ever to thrust hope upon him. What his love lacked in courage it made up in constancy, however, and morning, noon, and night—sometimes midnight too, I venture

The Solitary

to say—his all too patient heart had bowed
mutely down toward its holy city across the
burning sands of his diffidence. When another fellow stepped in and married her,
he simply loved on, in the same innocent,
dumb, harmless way as before. He gave
himself some droll consolations. One of
these was a pretty, sloop-rigged sail-boat,
trim and swift, on which he lavished the ten-
dernesses he knew he should never bestow
upon any living she. He named her Sweetheart; a general term; but he knew that we
all knew it meant the mender of his coat.
By and by his visits fell off and I met him
oftenest on the street. Sometimes we
stopped for a moment's sidewalk chat, New
Orleans fashion, and I still envied the clear
bronze of his fine skin, which the rest of us
had soon lost. But after a while certain
changes began to show for the worse, until
one day in the summer of the fifth year he
tried to hurry by me. I stopped him, and
was thinking what a handsome fellow he
was even yet, with such a quiet, modest
fineness about him, when he began, with a
sudden agony of face, " My schooner's sold

for debt! You know the reason; I've seen you read it all over me every time we have met, these twelve months—O *don't* look at me!"

His slim, refined hands—he gave me both —were clammy and tremulous. "Yes," he babbled on, "it's a fixed fact, Smith; the cracked fiddle's a smashed fiddle at last!"

I drew him out of the hot sun and into a secluded archway, he talking straight on with a speed and pitiful grandiloquence totally unlike him. "I've finished all the easy parts—the first ecstasies of pure license —the long down-hill plunge, with all its mad exhilarations—the wild vanity of venturing and defying—that bigness of the soul's experiences which makes even its anguish seem finer than the old bitterness of tame propriety—they are all behind me, now— the valley of horrors is before! You can't understand it, Smith. O you can't understand——"

O couldn't I! And, anyhow, one does not have to put himself through a whole criminal performance to apprehend its spiritual experiences. I understood all, and especially what he unwittingly betrayed even now; that deep thirst for the dramatic element in one's own life, which, when so-cial conformity fails to supply it, becomes, to an eager soul, sin's cunningest allurement.

I tried to talk to him. " Gregory, that day the dogs jumped on you—you remem-ber?—didn't you say if ever you should reach this condition your fear might save you? "

He stared at me a moment. " Do you "—a ray of humor lighted his eyes—" do you still believe in spasms of virtue? "

" Thank heaven, yes! " laughed I.

" Good-by," he said, and was gone.

I heard of him twice afterward that day. About noon some one coming into the of-fice said: " I just now saw Crackedfiddle buying a great lot of powder and shot and fishing-tackle. Here's a note. He says first read it and then seal it and send it to his aunt." It read:

" *Don't look for me. You can't find me. I'm not going to kill or hurt myself, and I'll report again in a month.*"

I delivered it in person on my way up-

town, advising his kinswoman to trust him
on his own terms and hope for the best.
Privately, of course, I was distressed, and
did not become less so when, on reaching
home, Mrs. Smith told me that he had been
there and borrowed an arm-load of books,
saying he might return some of them in
a month, but would probably keep others
for two. So he did; and one evening, when
he brought the last of them back, he told
us fully, spiritual experiences and all, what
had occurred to him in the interval.

The sale of the schooner had paid its debt
and left him some cash over. Better yet,
it had saved Sweetheart. On the day of his
disappearance she was lying at the head of
the New Basin, distant but a few minutes'
walk from the spot where we met and
talked. When he left me he went there.
At the stores thereabout he bought a new
hatchet and axe, an extra water-keg or two,
and a month's provisions. He filled all the
kegs, stowed everything aboard, and by the
time the afternoon had half waned was
rippling down the New Canal under mule-
tow with a strong lake breeze in his face.

The Solitary

At the lake (Pontchartrain), as the tow-line was cast off, he hoisted sail, and, skimming out by lighthouse and breakwater, tripped away toward Pointe-aux-Herbes and the eastern skyline beyond, he and Sweetheart alone, his hand clasping hers—the tiller, that is—hour by hour, and the small waves tiptoeing to kiss her southern cheek as she leaned the other away from the saucy north wind. In time the low land, and then the lighthouse, sank and vanished behind them; on the left the sun went down in the purple-black swamps of Manchac; the intervening waters turned crimson and bronze under the fairer changes of the sky, while in front of them Fort Pike Light began to glimmer through an opal haze, and by and by to draw near. It passed. From a large inbound schooner gliding by in the twilight, came in friendly recognition, the drone of a conch-shell, the last happy salutation Sweetheart was ever to receive. Then the evening star silvered their wake through the deep Rigolets, and the rising moon met them, her and her lover, in Lake Borgne, passing the dark pines of Round

Island, and hurrying on toward the white sand-keys of the Gulf.

The night was well advanced as they neared the pine-crested dunes of Cat Island, in whose lee a more cautious sailor would have dropped anchor till the morning. But to this pair every mile of these fickle waters, channel and mud-lump, snug lagoon, open sea and hidden bar, each and all, were known as the woods are known to a hunter, and, as he drew her hand closer to his side, she turned across the track of the moon and bounded into the wide south. A maze of marsh islands—huddling along that narrow, half-drowned mainland of cypress swamp and trembling prairie which follows the Mississippi out to sea—slept, leagues away, below the western waters. In the east lay but one slender boundary between the voyager and the shoreless deep, and this was so near that from its farther edge came now and again its admonishing murmur, the surf-thunder of the open Gulf rolling forever down the prone but unshaken battle-front of the sandy Chandeleurs.

The Solitary

IV

So all night, lest wind or resolve should fail next day, he sailed. How to tell just where dawn found him I scarcely know.

Somewhere in that blue wilderness, with no other shore in sight, yet not over three miles northeast of a " pass " between two long tide-covered sand-reefs, a ferment of delta silt—if science guesses right—had lifted higher than most of the islands behind it in the sunken west one mere islet in the shape of a broad crescent, with its outward curve to seaward and a deep, slender lagoon on the landward side filling the whole length of its bight. About half the island was flat and was covered with those strong marsh grasses for which you've seen cattle, on the mainland, venture so hungrily into the deep ooze. The rest, the southern half, rose in dazzling white dunes twenty feet or more in height and dappled green with patches of ragged sod and thin groups of dwarfed and wind-flattened shrubs. As the sun rose, Sweetheart and her sailor

glided through a gap in the sand reef that
closed the lagoon in, luffed, and as a great
cloud of nesting pelicans rose from their
dirty town on the flats, ran softly upon the
inner sands, where a rillet, a mere thread
of sweet water, trickled across the white
beach. Here he waded ashore with the
utensils and provisions, made a fire, washed
down a hot breakfast of bacon and pone
with a pint of black coffee, returned to his
boat and slept until afternoon. Wakened
at length by the canting of the sloop with
the fall of the tide, he rose, rekindled his
fire, cooked and ate again, smoked two
pipes, and then, idly shouldering his gun,
made a long half-circuit of the beach to
south and eastward, mounted the highest
dune and gazed far and wide.

Nowhere on sand or sea under the illim-
itable dome was there sign of human presence on the earth. Nor would there likely
be any. Except by misadventure no ship
on any course ever showed more than a
topmast above this horizon. Of the hunters
and fishermen who roamed the islands
nearer shore, with the Chandeleurs, the

storm-drowned Grand Gosiers and the deep-sea fishing grounds beyond, few knew the way hither, and fewer ever sailed it. At the sound of his gun the birds of the beach —sea-snipe, curlew, plover—showed the whites of their wings for an instant and fell to feeding again. Save when the swift Wilderness—you remember the revenue cutter —chanced this way on her devious patrol, only the steamer of the light-house inspection service, once a month, came up out of the southwest through yonder channel and passed within hail on her way from the stations of the Belize to those of Mississippi Sound; and he knew—had known before he left the New Basin—that she had just gone by here the day before.

But to Gregory this solitude brought no quick distress. With a bird or two at his belt he turned again toward his dying fire. Once on the way he paused, as he came in sight of the sloop, and gazed upon it with a faintness of heart he had not known since his voyage began. However, it presently left him, and hurrying down to her side he began to unload her completely, and to

make a permanent camp in the lee of a ridge
of sand crested with dwarfed casino bushes,
well up from the beach. The night did not
stop him, and by the time he was tired
enough for sleep he had lightened the boat
of everything stowed into her the previous
day. Before sunrise he was at work again,
removing her sandbags, her sails, flags,
cordage, even her spars. The mast would
have been heavy for two men to handle,
but he got it out whole, though not without
hurting one hand so painfully that he had
to lie off for over two hours. But by mid-
day he was busy again, and when at low
water poor Sweetheart comfortably turned
upon her side on the odorous, clean sand, it
was never more to rise. The keen, new axe
of her master ended her days.

"No! O no!" he said to me, "call it
anything but courage! I felt—I don't want
to be sentimental—I'm sure I was not sentimental at the time, but—I felt as though
I were a murderer. All I knew was that it
had to be done. I trembled like a thief.
I had to stoop twice before I could take up
the axe, and I was so cold my teeth chat-

tered. When I lifted the first blow I didn't
know where it was going to fall. But it
struck as true as a die, and then I flew at
it. I never chopped so fast or clean in my
life. I wasn't fierce; I was as full of self-
delight as an overpraised child. And yet
when something delayed me an instant I
found I was still shaking. Courage," said
he, " O no; I know what it was, and I knew
then. But I had no choice; it was my last
chance."

I told him that anyone might have
thought him a madman chopping up his
last chance.

" Maybe so," he replied, " but I wasn't;
it was the one sane thing I could do; " and
he went on to tell me that when night fell
the tallest fire that ever leapt from those
sands blazed from Sweetheart's piled ribs
and keel.

It was proof to him of his having been
shrewd, he said, that for many days he felt
no repentance of the act nor was in the least
lonely. There was an infinite relief merely
in getting clean away from the huge world
of men, with all its exactions and tempta-

tions and the myriad rebukes and rebuffs
of its crass propriety and thrift. He had
endured solitude enough in it; the secret
loneliness of a spiritual bankruptcy. Here
was life begun over, with none to make new
debts to except nature and himself, and no
besetments but his own circumvented pro-
pensities. What humble, happy master-
hood! Each dawn he rose from dreamless
sleep and leaped into the surf as into the
embrace of a new existence. Every hour
of day brought some unfretting task or hale
pastime. With sheath-knife and sail-needle
he made of his mainsail a handsome tent,
using the mainboom for his ridge-pole, and
finishing it just in time for the first night of
rain—when, nevertheless, he lost all his
coffee!

He did not waste toil. He hoarded its
opportunities as one might husband salt on
the mountains or water in the desert, and
loitering in well calculated idleness between
thoughts many and things of sea and shore
innumerable, filled the intervals from labor
to labor with gentle entertainment. Sky-
ward ponderings by night, canny discov-

The Solitary

eries under foot by day, quickened his mind
and sight to vast and to minute significan-
cies, until they declared an Author known
to him hitherto only by tradition. Every
acre of the barren islet grew fertile in beauties and mysteries, and a handful of sand at
the door of his tent held him for hours
guessing the titanic battles that had ground
the invincible quartz to that crystal meal
and fed it to the sea.

I may be more rhetorical than he was,
but he made all the more of these condi-
tions while experiencing them, because he
knew they could not last out the thirty days,
nor half the thirty, and took modest comfort in a will strong enough to meet all
present demands, well knowing there was
one exigency yet to arise, one old usurer
still to be settled with who had not yet
brought in his dun.

V

IT came—began to come—in the middle of the second week. At its familiar approach he felt no dismay, save a certain inert dismay that it brought none. Three, four, five times he went bravely to the rill, drowned his thirst and called himself satisfied; but the second day was worse than the first; the craving seemed better than the rill's brief cure of it, and once he rose straight from drinking of the stream and climbed the dune to look for a sail.

He strove in vain to labor. The pleasures of toil were as stale as those of idleness. His books were put aside with a shudder, and he walked abroad with a changed gait; the old extortioner was levying on his nerves. And on his brain. He dreamed that night of war times; found himself commander of a whole battery of heavy guns, and lo, they were all quaker cannon. When he would have fled, monstrous terrors met him at every turn, till he woke and could sleep no more. Dawn widened over sky

The Solitary

and sea, but its vast beauty only mocked the castaway. All day long he wandered up and down and along and across his glittering prison, no tiniest speck of canvas, no faintest wreath of smoke, on any water's edge; the horror of his isolation growing —growing—like the monsters of his dream, and his whole nature wild with a desire which was no longer a mere physical drought, but a passion of the soul, that gave the will an unnatural energy and set at naught every true interest of earth and heaven. Again and again he would have shrieked its anguish, but the first note of his voice rebuked him to silence as if he had espied himself in a glass. He fell on his face voiceless, writhing, and promised himself, nay, pledged creation and its Creator, that on the day of his return to the walks of men he would drink the cup of madness and would drink it thenceforth till he died.

When night came again he paced the sands for hours and then fell to work to drag by long and toiling zigzags to a favorable point on the southern end of the island the mast he had saved, and to raise there a flag of distress. In the shortness of his resources he dared not choose the boldest exposures, where the first high wind would cast it down; but where he placed it it could be seen from every quarter except the north, and any sail approaching from that direction was virtually sure to come within hail even of the voice.

Day had come again as he left the finished task, and once more from the highest wind-built ridge his hungering eyes swept the round sea's edge. But he saw no sail. Nerveless and exhausted he descended to the southeastern beach and watched the morning brighten. The breezes, that for some time had slept, fitfully revived, and the sun leaped from the sea and burned its way through a low bank of dark and ruddy clouds with so unusual a splendor that the beholder was in some degree both quickened and tranquillized. He could even play at self-command, and in child fashion bound himself not to mount the dunes again for a northern look within an hour. This southern half-circle must suffice. Indeed, unless these idle zephyrs should amend, no sail could in that time draw near enough to notice any signal he could offer.

Playing at self-command gave him some earnest of it. In a whim of the better man he put off his clothes and sprang into the breakers. He had grown chill, but a long wrestle with the surf warmed his blood, and as he reclothed himself and with a better step took his way along the beach toward his tent a returning zest of manhood refreshed his spirit. The hour was up, but in a kind of equilibrium of impulses and with much emptiness of mind, he let it lengthen on, made a fire, and for the first time in two days cooked food. He ate and still tarried. A brand in his camp fire, a piece from the remnant of his boat, made beautiful flames. He idly cast in another and was pleased to find himself sitting there instead of gazing his eyes out for sails that never rose into view. He watched a third brand smoke and blaze. And then, as tamely as if the new impulse were only another part of a continued abstraction, he arose and once more climbed the sandy hills. The highest was some distance from his camp. At one point near its top a brief northeastward glimpse of the marsh's outer edge and the blue waters beyond showed at least that nothing had come near enough to raise the pelicans. But the instant his sight cleared the crown of the ridge he rushed forward, threw up his arms, and lifted his voice in a long, imploring yell. Hardly two miles away, her shapely canvas leaning and stiffening in the augmented breeze, a small yacht had just gone about, and with twice the speed at which she must have approached was hurrying back straight into the north.

The frantic man dashed back and forth along the crest, tossing his arms, waving his Madras handkerchief, cursing himself for leaving his gun so far behind, and again and again repeating his vain ahoys in wilder and wilder alternations of beseeching and rage. The lessening craft flew straight on, no ear in her skilled enough to catch the distant cry, and no eye alert enough to scan the dwindling sand-hills. He ceased to call, but still, with heavy notes of distress to him-

self, waved and waved, now here, now there,
while the sail grew smaller and smaller. At
length he stopped this also and only stood
gazing. Almost on first sight of the craft
he had guessed that the men in her had
taken alarm at the signs of changing
weather, and seeing the freshening smoke
of his fire had also inferred that earlier
sportsmen were already on the island. Oh,
if he could have fired one shot when she
was nearest! But already she was as hopelessly gone as though she were even now
below the horizon. Suddenly he turned and
ran down to his camp. Not for the gun;
not in any new hope of signalling the yacht.
No, no; a raft! a raft! Deliverance or destruction, it should be at his own hand and
should wait no longer!

A raft forthwith he set about to make.
Some stout portions of his boat were still
left. Tough shrubs of the sand-hills furnished trennels and suppler parts. Of ropes
there was no lack. The mast was easily
dragged down again to the beach to be once
more a mast, and in nervous haste, yet with
skill and thoroughness, the tent was ripped

up and remade into a sail, and even a rude centreboard was rigged in order that one might tack against unfavorable winds.

Winds, at nightfall, when the thing began to be near completion, there were none. The day's sky had steadily withdrawn its favor. The sun shone as it sank into the waves, but in the northwest and southeast dazzling thunderheads swelled from the sea's line high into the heavens, and in the early dusk began with silent kindlings to challenge each other to battle. As night swiftly closed down the air grew unnaturally still. From the toiler's brow, worse than at noon, the sweat rolled off, as at last he brought his work to a close by the glare of his leaping camp-fire. Now, unless he meant only to perish, he must once more eat and sleep while he might. Then let the storm fall; the moment it was safely over and the wind in the right quarter he would sail. As for the thirst which had been such a torture while thwarted, now that it ruled unchallenged, it was purely a wild, glad zeal as full of method as of diligence. But first he must make his diminished pro-

The Solitary

visions and his powder safe against the elements; and this he did, covering them with
a waterproof stuff and burying them in a
northern slope of sand.

He awoke in the small hours of the night.
The stars of the zenith were quenched.
Blackness walled and roofed him in close
about his crumbled fire, save when at shorter and shorter intervals and with more and
more deafening thunders the huge clouds
lit up their own forms, writhing one upon
another, and revealed the awe-struck sea
and ghostly sands waiting breathlessly below. He rose to lay on more fuel, and while
he was in the act the tornado broke upon
him. The wind, as he had forecast, came
out of the southeast. In an instant it was
roaring and hurtling against the farther
side of his island rampart like the charge of
a hundred thousand horse and tossing the
sand of the dunes like blown hair into the
northwest, while the rain in one wild deluge
lashed the frantic sea and weltering lagoon
as with the whips of the Furies.

He had kept the sail on the beach for
a protection from the storm, but before he
could crawl under it he was as wet as though

he had been tossed up by the deep, and yet was glad to gain its cover from the blinding floods and stinging sand. Here he lay for more than an hour, the rage of the tempest continually growing, the heavens in a constant pulsing glare of lightnings, their terrific thunders smiting and bellowing round and round its echoing vault, and the very island seeming at times to stagger back and recover again as it braced itself against the fearful onsets of the wind. Snuggling in his sailcloth burrow, he complacently recalled an earlier storm like this, which he and Sweetheart, the only other time they ever were here, had tranquilly weathered in this same lagoon. On the mainland, in that storm, cane- and rice-fields had been laid low and half destroyed, houses had been unroofed, men had been killed. A woman and a boy, under a pecan tree, were struck by lightning; and three men who had covered themselves with a tarpaulin on one of the wharves in New Orleans were blown with it into the Mississippi, poor fellows, and were drowned; a fact worthy of second consideration in the present juncture.

The Solitary

This second thought had hardly been given it before he crept hastily from his refuge and confronted the gale in quick alarm. The hurricane was veering to southward. Let it shift but a point or two more, and its entire force would sweep the lagoon and its beach. Before long the change came. The mass of canvas at his feet leapt clear of the ground and fell two or three yards away. He sprang to seize it, but in the same instant the whole storm—rain, wind, and sand—whirled like a troop of fiends round the southern end of the island, the ceaseless lightnings showing the way, and came tearing and howling up its hither side. The white sail lifted, bellied, rolled, fell, vaulted into the air, fell again, tumbled on, and at the foot of a dune stopped until its wind-buffeted pursuer had almost overtaken it. Then it fled again, faster, faster, higher, higher up the sandy slope to its top, caught and clung an instant on some unseen bush, and then with one mad bound into the black sky, unrolled, widened like a phantom, and vanished forever.

Gregory turned in desperation, and in the

glare of the lightning looked back toward his raft. Great waves were rolling along and across the slender reef in wide obliques and beating themselves to death in the lagoon, or sweeping out of it again seaward at its more northern end. On the dishevelled crest of one he saw his raft, and on another its mast. He could not look a second time. The flying sand blinded him and cut the blood from his face. He could only cover his eyes and crawl under the bushes in such poor lee as he could find; and there, with the first lull of the storm, heavy with exhaustion and despair, he fell asleep and slept until far into the day. When he awoke the tempest was over.

Even more completely the tumult within him was quieted. He rose and stood forth mute in spirit as in speech; humbled, yet content, in the consciousness that having miserably failed first to save himself and then to rue himself back to destruction, the hurricane had been his deliverer. It had spared his supplies, his ammunition, his weapons, only hiding them deeper under the dune sands; but scarce a vestige of his camp

38

remained and of his raft nothing. As once
more from the highest sand-ridge he looked
down upon the sea weltering in the majestic
after-heavings of its passion, at the eastern
beach booming under the shock of its lofty
rollers, and then into the sky still gray with
the endless flight of southward-hurrying
scud, he felt the stir of a new attachment to
them and his wild prison, and pledged al-
liance with them thenceforth.

VI

HERE, in giving me his account, Gregory
asked me if that sounded sentimental. I
said no, and thereupon he actually tried to
apologize to me as though I were a pro-
fessional story-teller, for having had so few
deep feelings in the moments where the ro-
mancists are supposed to place them. I told
him what I had once seen a mechanic do
on a steep, slated roof nearly a hundred
feet from the pavement. He had faced
around from his work, which was close to
the ridge-tiles, probably to kick off the

shabby shoes he had on, when some hold failed him and he began to slide toward the eaves. We people in the street below fairly moaned our horror, but he didn't utter a sound. He held back with all his skill, one leg thrust out in front, the other drawn up with the knee to his breast, and his hands flattened beside him on the slates, but he came steadily on down till his forward foot passed over the eaves and his heel caught on the tin gutter. Then he stopped. We held our breath below. He slowly and cautiously threw off one shoe, then the other, and then turned, climbed back up the roof and resumed his work. And we two or three witnesses down in the street didn't think any less of him because he did so without any show of our glad emotion.

"O, if I had that fellow's nerve," said Gregory, "that would be another thing!"

My wife and I smiled at each other. "How would it be 'another thing?'" we asked. "Did *you* not quietly get up and begin life over again as if nothing had occurred?"

"There wasn't anything else to do," he

replied, with a smile. " The feelings came later, too, in an easy sort o' gradual way. I never could quite make out how men get such clear notions of what they call ' Providence,' but, just the same, I know by experience there's all the difference of peace and misery, or life and death, whether you're in partnership with the things that help the world on, or with those that hold it back."

" But with that feeling," my wife asked, " did not your longing for our human world continue? "

" No," he replied, " but I got a new liking for it—although, you understand, *I* never had anything against *it*, of course. It's too big and strong for me, that's all; and that's my fault. Your man on that slippery roof kicking his shoes off is a sort of parable to me. If your hand or your foot offend you and you have to cut it off, that's a physical disablement, and bad enough. But when your gloves and your shoes are too much for you, and you have to pluck *them* off and cast them from you, you find each one is a great big piece of the civilized world, and you hardly know how much you did like it, till you've lost it. And still, it's no use longing, when you know your limitations, and I saw I'd got to keep *my* world trimmed down to where I could run barefooted on the sand."

He told us that now he began for the first time since coming to the island, to find his books his best source of interest and diversion. He learned, he said, a way of reading by which sea, sky, book, island, and absent humanity, all seemed parts of one whole, and all to speak together in one harmony, while they toiled together for one harmony some day to be perfected. Not all books, nor even all good books, were equally good for that effect, he thought, and the best——

"You might not think it," he said, "but the best was a Bible I'd chanced to carry along;" he didn't know precisely what kind, but "just one of these ordinary Bibles you see lying around in people's houses." He extolled the psalms and asked Mrs. Smith if she'd ever noticed the beauty of the twenty-third. She smiled and said she believed she had.

The Solitary

" Then there was one," he went on, " beginning, ' Lord, my heart is not haughty,
nor mine eyes lofty; neither do I exercise
myself in great matters, or in things too
wonderful for me;' and by and by it says,
' Surely, I have quieted myself as a child
that is weaned: my soul is even as a weaned
child.' "

One day, after a most marvellous sunset,
he had been reading, he said, " that long
psalm with twenty-two parts in it—a hundred and seventy-six verses." He had intended to read " Lord, my heart is not
haughty " after it, though the light was fast
failing, but at the hundred and seventy-
sixth verse he closed the book. Thus he sat
in the nearly motionless air, gazing on the
ripples of the lagoon as, now singly, and
now by twos or threes, they glided up the
beach tinged with the colors of parting day
as with a grace of resignation, and sank
into the grateful sands like the lines of this
last verse sinking into his heart; now singly
—" I have gone astray like a lost sheep;"
and now by twos—" I have gone astray like
a lost sheep; save thy servant;" or by

threes—" I have gone astray like a lost
sheep; save thy servant; for I do not forget
thy commandments."

" I shouldn't tell that," he said to us,
" if I didn't know so well how little it
counts for. But I knew at the time that
when the next day but one should bring
the lighthouse steamer I shouldn't be any
more fit to go ashore, *to stay*, than a jelly-
fish." We agreed, he and I that there
can be as wide a distance between fine
feelings and faithful doing as, he said, " between listening to the band and charging
a battery."

On the islet the night deepened. The
moon had not risen, and the stars only
glorified the dark, as it, in turn, revealed
the unearthly beauties of a phosphorescent
sea. It was one of those rare hours in which
the deep confessed the amazing numbers of
its own living and swarming constellations.
Not a fish could leap or dart, not a sinuous
thing could turn, but it became an animate
torch. Every quick movement was a gleam
of green fire. No drifting, flaccid life could
pulse so softly along but it betrayed itself

in lambent outlines. Each throb of the water became a beam of light, and every ripple that widened over the strand—still whispering, "I have gone astray"—was edged with luminous pearls.

In an agreeable weariness of frame, untroubled in mind, and counting the night too beautiful for slumber he reclined on the dry sands with an arm thrown over a small pile of fagots which he had spent the day in gathering from every part of the island to serve his need for the brief remainder of his stay. In this search he had found but one piece of his boat, a pine board. This he had been glad to rive into long splinters and bind together again as a brand, with which to signal the steamer if—contrary to her practice, I think he said—she should pass in the night. And so, without a premonition of drowsiness, he was presently asleep, with the hours radiantly folding and expiring one upon another like the ripples on the beach.

When he came to himself he was on his feet. The moon was high, his fire was smouldering; his heart was beating madly and his eyes were fixed on the steamer, looming large, moving at full speed, her green light showing, her red light hid, and her long wake glowing with comet fire. In a moment she would be passing. It was too late for beacon-flame or torch. He sprang for his gun, and mounting the first low rise fired into the air, once!—twice!—and shouted, " Help!—help! "

She kept straight on. She was passing, she was passing! In trembling haste he loaded and fired again, again wailed out his cry for help, and still she kept her speed. He had loaded for the third discharge, still frantically calling the while, and was lifting his gun to fire when he saw the white light at her foremast-head begin to draw nearer to the green light at her waist and knew she was turning. He fired, shouted, and tried to load again ; but as her red light brightened into view beside the green, he dropped his gun and leaped and crouched and laughed and wept for joy.

" Why, Gregory! " the naval lieutenant cried, as the castaway climbed from the steamer's boat to her deck. "Why, you blasted old cracked fiddle! what in——"

"Right, the first guess!" laughed Gregory, "there's where I've been!" and in the cabin he explained all.

"The fiddle's mended," he concluded. "You can play a tune on it—by being careful."

"But what's your tune?" asked his hearer; "you cannot go back to that island."

"Yes, I'll be on it in a week—with a schooner-load of cattle. I can get them on credit. Going to raise cattle there as a regular business. They'll fatten in that marsh like blackbirds."

True enough, before the week was up the mended fiddle was playing its tune. It was not until Gregory's second return from his island that he came to see us and told us his simple story. We asked him how it was that the steamer, that first time, had come so much earlier than she generally did.

"She didn't," he replied. "I had miscounted one day."

"Don't you," asked my wife, who would

have liked a more religious tone in Gregory's recital, "don't you have trouble to keep run of your Sabbaths away out there alone?"

"Why"—he smiled—"it's always Sunday there. Here almost everybody feels duty bound to work harder than somebody else, or else make somebody else work harder than he, and you need a day every now and then for Sunday—or Sabbath, at least. Oh, I suppose it's all one in the end, isn't it? You take your's in a pill, I take mine in a powder. Not that it's the least bit like a dose, however, except for the good it does."

"And you're really prospering, even in a material way!" I said.

"Yes," he answered. "O yes; the island's already too small for us."

"It's certainly very dangerously exposed," said my wife, and I guessed her thought was on Last Island, which, you remember, though very large and populous, had been, within our recollection, totally submerged, with dreadful loss of life.

"O yes," he responded, "there's always

48

something wherever you are. One of these days some storm's going to roll the sea clean over the whole thing."

"Then, why don't you move to a bigger island closer inshore?" she asked.

"I'm afraid," said Gregory, and smiled.

"Afraid!" said my wife, incredulously.

"Yes," he responded. "I'm afraid my prisoner'll get away from me."

As his hand closed over hers in good-by I saw, what he could not, that she had half a notion to kiss it. I told her so when he was gone, and kissed hers—for him.

"I don't care," she said, dreamily, as it lingered in mine, "I'm glad I mended his coat for him that time."

The Taxidermist

The Taxidermist

ONE day a hummingbird got caught in a cobweb in our greenhouse. It had no real need to seek that damp, artificial heat. We were in the very heart of that Creole summer-time when bird-notes are many as the sunbeams. The flowers were in such multitude they seemed to follow one about, offering their honeys and perfumes and begging to be gathered. Our little boy saw the embodied joy fall, a joy no longer, seized it, and clasping it too tightly, brought it to me dead.

He cried so over the loss that I promised to have the body stuffed. This is how I came to know Manouvrier, the Taxidermist in St. Peter Street.

I passed his place twice before I found it. The front shop was very small, dingily clean and scornfully unmercantile. Of the very few specimens of his skill to be seen round about not one was on parade, yet everyone was somehow an achievement, a happy surprise, a lasting delight. I admit that taxidermy is not classed among the fine arts; but you know there is a way of making everything—anything—an art instead of a craft or a commerce, and such was the way of this shop's big, dark, hairy-faced, shaggy-headed master. I saw his unsmiling face soften and his eye grow kind as mine lighted up with approbation of his handiwork.

When I handed him the hummingbird he held it tenderly in his wide palm, and as I was wondering to myself how so huge a hand as that could manipulate frail and tiny things and bring forth delicate results, he looked into my face and asked, with a sort of magisterial gentleness:

" How she git kill', dat lill' bird? "

I told him. I could feel my mood and words take their tone from him, though he outwardly heard me through with no show of feeling; and when I finished, I knew we were friends. I presently ventured to praise

54

The Taxidermist

the specimen of his skill nearest at hand; a wild turkey listening alarmedly as if it would the next instant utter that ringing "quit!" which makes each separate drop of a hunter's blood tingle. But with an odd languor in his gravity, he replied:

"Naw, dass not well make; lill' bit worse, bad enough to put in front window. I take you inside; come."

II

WE passed through into a private workroom immediately behind the shop. His wife sat there sewing; a broad, motherly woman of forty-five, fat, tranquil, kind, with an old eye, a young voice, and a face that had got its general flabbiness through much paddling and gnawing from other women's teething babes. She sat still, unintroduced, but welcomed me with a smile.

I was saying to her husband that a hummingbird was a very small thing to ask him to stuff. But he stopped me with his lifted palm.

"My fran', a hummingbird has de pas-
sione'—de ecstacie! One drop of blood wid
the pas-sione in it"—He waved his hand
with a jerk of the thumb in disdain of
spoken words, and it was I who added,

"Is bigger than the sun?"

"Hah!" was all he uttered in approval,
turning as if to go to work. I feared I had
disappointed him.

"God measures by the soul, not by the
size," I suggested. But he would say no
more, and his wife put in as softly as a kettle
beginning to sing,

"Ah, ha, ha! I t'ink dass where de good
God show varrie good sanse."

I began looking here and there in earti-
est admiration of the products of his art
and presently we were again in full sympathy and talking eagerly. As I was going
he touched my arm:

"You will say de soul is parted from dat
lill' bird. And—yass; but "—he let a gest-
ure speak the rest.

"I know," replied I; "you propose to
make the soul seem to come back and leave
us its portrait. I believe you will." Where-

upon he gave me his first, faint smile, and detained me with another touch.

"Msieu Smeet; when you was bawn?"

"I? December 9, 1844. Why do you ask?"

"O nut'n'; only I thing you make me luck; nine, h-cighteen, fawty-fo'—I play me doze number' in de lott'ree to-day."

"Why, pshaw! you don't play the lottery, do you?"

"Yass. I play her; why not? She make me reech some of doze day'. Win fifty dollah one time las' year."

The soft voice of the wife spoke up— "And spend it all to the wife of my dead brother. What use him be reech? I think he don't stoff bird' no bettch."

But the husband responded more than half to himself,

"Yass, I think mebbe I stoff him lill' more betteh."

When, some days afterward I called again, thinking as I drew near how much fineness of soul and life, seen or unseen, must have existed in earlier generations to have produced this man, I noticed the in-

conspicuous sign over his door, P. T. B.
Manouvrier, and as he led me at once into
the back room I asked him playfully what
such princely abundance of initials might
stand for.

" Doze? Ah, doze make only Pas-Trop-
Bon."

I appealed to his wife; but she, with her
placid laugh, would only confirm him:

" Yass; Pastropbon; he like that name.
Tha's all de way I call him—Pastropbon."

III

THE hummingbird was ready for me. I
will not try to tell how lifelike and beautiful the artist had made it. Even with him
I took pains to be somewhat reserved. As
I stood holding and admiring the small
green wonder, I remarked that I was near
having to bring him that morning another
and yet finer bird. A shade of displeasure
(and, I feared, of suspicion also) came to
his face as he asked me how that was. I
explained.

The Taxidermist

Going into my front hall, whose veranda-door framed in a sunny picture of orange-boughs, jasmine-vines, and white-clouded blue sky, I had found a male ruby-throat circling about the ceiling, not wise enough to stoop, fly low, and pass out by the way it had come in. It occurred to me that it might be the mate of the one already mine. For some time all the efforts I could contrive, either to capture or free it, were vain. Round and round it flew, silently beating and bruising its exquisite little head against the lofty ceiling, the glory of its luminous red throat seeming to heighten into an expression of unspeakable agony. At last Mrs. Smith ran for a long broom, and, as in her absence I stood watching the self-snared captive's struggle, the long, tiny beak which had never done worse than go twittering with rapture to the grateful hearts of thousands of flowers, began to trace along the smooth, white ceiling a scarlet thread of pure heart's blood. The broom came. I held it up, the flutterer lighted upon it, and at first slowly, warily, and then triumphantly, I lowered it under

59

the lintel out into the veranda, and the bird
darted away into the garden and was gone
like a soul into heaven.

In the middle of my short recital Manouvrier had sunk down upon the arm of
his wife's rocking-chair with one huge hand
on both of hers folded over her sewing, and
as I finished he sat motionless, still gazing
into my face.

"But," I started, with sudden pretence
of business impulse, "how much am I to
pay?"

He rose, slowly, and looked dreamily at
his wife; she smiled at him, and he grunted,
"Nut'n'."

"Oh, my friend," I laughed, "that's
absurd!"

But he had no reply, and his wife, as
she resumed her sewing, said, sweetly, as
if to her needle, "Ah, I think Pastropbon
don't got to charge nut'n' if he don't feel
like." And I could not move them.

As I was leaving them, a sudden con-
jecture came to me.

"Did those birthday numbers bring you
any luck?"

The Taxidermist

The taxidermist shook his head, good-naturedly, but when his wife laughed he turned upon her.

"Wait! I dawn't be done wid doze number' yet."

I guessed that, having failed with them in the daily drawings, he would shift the figures after some notion of magical significance and venture a ticket, whole or fractional, in the monthly drawing.

Scarcely ten days after, as I sat at breakfast with my newspaper spread beside my plate, I fairly spilled my coffee as my eye fell upon the name of P. T. B. Manouvrier, of No. — St. Peter Street. Old Pastropbon had drawn seventy-five thousand dollars in the lottery.

IV

ALL the first half of the day, wherever I was, in the street-car, at my counting-desk, on the exchange, no matter to what I gave my attention, my thought was ever on my friend the taxidermist. At luncheon it was the same. He was rich! And what, now? What next? And what—ah! what —at last? Would the end be foul or fair? I hoped, yet feared. I feared again; and yet I hoped.

A familiar acquaintance, a really good fellow, decent, rich, "born of pious parents," and determined to have all the ready-made refinements and tastes that pure money could buy, came and sat with me at my lunch table.

"I wonder," he began, "if you know where you are, or what you're here for. I've been watching you for five minutes and I don't believe you do. See here; what sort of an old donkey is that bird-stuffer of yours?"

The Taxidermist

"You know, then, his good fortune of yesterday, do you?"

"No, I don't. I know my bad fortune with him last week."

I dropped my spoon into my soup. "Why, what?"

"Oh, no great shakes. Only, I went to his place to buy that wild turkey you told me about. I wanted to stand it away up on top of that beautiful old carved buffet I picked up in England last year. I was fully prepared to buy it on your say-so, but, all the same, I saw its merits the moment I set eyes on it. It has but one fault; did you notice that? I don't believe you did. I pointed it out to him."

"You pointed—what did he say?"

"He said I was right."

"Why, what was the fault?"

"Fault? Why, the perspective is bad; not exactly bad, but poor; lacks richness and rhythm."

"And yet you bought the thing."

"No, I didn't."

"You didn't buy it?"

"No, sir, I didn't buy it. I began by

pricing three or four other things first, so he couldn't know which one to stick the fancy price on to, and incidentally I thought I would tell him—you'd told me, you remember, how your accounts of your two birds had warmed him up and melted his feelings——"

"I didn't tell you. My wife told your wife, and your wife, I——"

"Yes, yes. Well, anyhow, I thought I'd try the same game, so I told him how I had stuffed a bird once upon a time myself. It was a pigeon, with every feather as white as snow; a fan-tail. It had belonged to my little boy who died. I thought it would make such a beautiful emblem at his funeral, rising with wings outspread, you know, typical of the resurrection—we buried him from the Sunday-school, you remember. And so I killed it and wired it and stuffed it myself. It was hard to hang it in a soaring attitude, owing to its being a fan-tail, but I managed it."

"And you told that to Manouvrier! What did he say?"

"Say? He never so much as cracked a

64

smile. When I'd done he stood so still, looking at me, that I turned and sort o' stroked the turkey and said, jestingly, says I, ' How much a pound for this gobbler?' "

" That ought to have warmed him up."

" Well, it didn't. He smiled like a dancing-master, lifted my hand off the bird and says, says he, ' She's not for sale.' Then he turned to go into his back room and leave me standing there. Well, that warmed *me* up. Says I, ' What in thunder is it here for, then? and if it ain't for sale, come back here and show me what is!'

" ' Nawtin',' says 'e, with the same polite smile. ' Nawtin' for sale. I come back when you gone.' His voice was sweet as sugar, but he slammed the door. I would have followed him in and put some better manners into him with a kick, but the old orang-outang had turned the key inside, and when I'd had time to remember that I was a deacon and Sunday-school teacher I walked away. What do you mean by his good fortune of yesterday? "

" I mean he struck Charlie Howard for seventy-five thousand."

My hearer's mouth dropped open. He was equally amazed and amused. "Well, well, well! That accounts for his silly high-headedness."

"Ah! no: that matter of yours was last week and the drawing was only yesterday."

"Oh, that's so. I don't keep run of that horrible lottery business. It makes me sick at heart to see the hideous canker poisoning the character and blasting the lives of every class of our people—why, don't you think so?"

"Oh, yes, I—I do. Yes, I certainly do!"

"But your conviction isn't exactly red-hot, I perceive. Come, wake up."

We rose. At the first street corner, as we were parting, I noticed he was still talking of the lottery.

"Pestilential thing," he was calling it. "Men blame it lightly on the ground that there are other forms of gambling which our laws don't reach. I suppose a tiger in a village mustn't be killed till we have killed all the tigers back in the woods!"

I assented absently and walked away full

of a vague shame. For I know as well as anyone that a man without a quick, strong, aggressive, insistent indignation against undoubted evil is a very poor stick.

V

At dinner that evening, Mrs. Smith broke a long silence with the question:

" Did you go to see Manouvrier? "

" Nn—o."

She looked at me drolly. " Did you go half way and turn back? "

" Yes," said I, " that's precisely what I did." And we dropped the subject.

But in the night I felt her fingers softly touch my shoulder.

" Warm night," I remarked.

" Richard," said she, " it will be time enough to be troubled about your taxidermist when he's given you cause."

" I'm not troubled; I'm simply interested. I'll go down to-morrow and see him." A little later it rained, very softly, and straight down, so that there was no need to shut the windows, and I slept like an infant until the room was full of sunshine.

All the next day and evening, summer though it was and the levee and sugar-sheds and cotton-yards virtually empty, I was kept by unexpected business and could not go near St. Peter Street. Both my partners were away on their vacations. But on the third afternoon our office regained its summer quiet and I was driving my pen through the last matter that prevented my going where I pleased, when I was disturbed by the announcement of a visitor. I pushed my writing on to a finish though he stood just at my back. Then I turned to bid him talk fast as my time was limited, when who should it be but Manouvrier. I took him into my private office, gave him a chair and said:

" I was just coming to see you."

" You had somet'in' to git stoff'? "

" No; I—Oh, I didn't know but you might like to see me."

" Yass?—Well—yass. I wish you come yesterday."

68

The Taxidermist

"Indeed? Why so; to protect you from reporters and beggars?"

"Naw; my wife she keep off all doze Peter an' John. Naw; one man bring me one wile cat to stoff. Ah! a *so* fine as I never see! Beautiful like da dev'l! Since two day' an' night' I can't make out if I want to fix dat wile cat stan'in' up aw sittin' down!"

"Did you decide at last?"

"Yass, I dis-ide. How you think I dis-ide?"

"Ah! you're too hard for me. But one thing I know."

"Yass? What you know?"

"That you will never do so much to anything as to leave my imagination nothing to do. You will always give my imagination strong play and never a bit of hard work."

"Come! Come and see!"

I took my hat. "Is that what you called to see me about?"

"Ah!" He started in sudden recollection and brought forth the lottery company's certified check for the seventy-five thousand dollars. "You keep dat?—lill' while?—for me? Yass; till I mek out how I goin' to spend her."

"Manouvrier, may I make one condition?"

"Yass."

"It is that you will never play the lottery again."

"Ah! Yass, I play her ag'in! You want know whan ole Pastropbon play her ag'in? One doze fine mawning—mebbee—dat sun —going rise hisself in de wes'. Well: when ole Pastropbon see dat, he play dat lott'ree ag'in. But biffo' he see dat"— He flirted his thumb.

Not many days later a sudden bereavement brought our junior partner back from Europe and I took my family North for a more stimulating air. Before I went I called on my St. Peter Street friend to say that during my absence either of my partners would fulfil any wish of his concerning the money. In his wife's sewing-basket in the back room I noticed a batch of unopened letters, and ventured a question which had been in my mind for several days.

" Manouvrier, you must get a host of letters these days from people who think you ought to help them because you have got money and they haven't. Do you read them?"

" Naw!" He gave me his back, bending suddenly over some real or pretended work. " I read some—first day. Since dat time I give 'em to old woman—wash hand—go to work ag'in—naw use."

" Ah! no use?" piped up the soft-voiced wife. " I use them to light those fire to cook those soup." But I felt the absence of her accustomed laugh.

" Well, it's there whenever you want it," I said to the husband as I was leaving.

" What?" The tone of the response was harsh. " What is where?"

" Why, the money. It's in the bank."

" Hah!" he said, with a contemptuous smile and finished with his thumb. That was the first time I ever saw a thumb swear. But in a moment his kindly gravity was on him again and he said, " Daz all right; I come git her some day."

VI

I DID not get back to New Orleans till late in the fall. In the office they told me that Manouvrier had been in twice to see if I had returned, and they had promised to send him word of my arrival. But I said no, and went to see him.

I found new lines of care on his brow, but the old kindness was still in his eye. We exchanged a few words of greeting and inquiry, and then there came a pause, which I broke.

"Well, stuffing birds better than ever, I suppose."

"Naw," he looked around upon his work, "I dawn't think. I dunno if I stoff him quite so good like biffo'." Another pause. Then, "I think I mek out what I do wid doze money now."

"Indeed," said I, and noticed that his face was averted from his wife.

She lifted her eyes to his broad back with a quizzical smile, glanced at me knowingly,

and dropped them again upon her sewing,
sighed:

"Ah-bah!" Then she suddenly glanced
at me with a pretty laugh and added,
"Since all that time he dunno what he
goin' to make with it. If he trade with it I
thing he don't stoff bird no mo', and I
thing he lose it bis-ide—ha, ha, ha!—and if
he keep it all time lock in doze bank I thing
he jiz well not have it." She laughed again.

But he quite ignored her and resumed,
as if out of a revery, "Yass, at de las' I mek
dat out." And the wife interrupted him in
a tone that was like the content of a singing
hen.

"I think it don't worth while to leave it
to our chillun, en't it?"

"Ah!" said the husband, entirely to me,
"daz de troub'! You see?—we dawn't got
some ba-bee'! Dat neveh arrive to her.
God know' dass not de fault of us."

"Yass," put in his partner, smiling to
her needle, "the good God know' that verrie
well." And the pair exchanged a look of
dove-like fondness.

"Yass," Manouvrier mused aloud once

more, "I think I build my ole woman one fine house."

"Ah! I don't want!"

"But yass! Foudre tonnerre! how I goin' spend her else? w'iskee? hosses? women? what da dev'l! Naw, I build a fine 'ouse. You see! she want dat house bad enough when she see her. Yass; fifty t'ousan' dollah faw house and twenty-five t'ousan' "—he whisked his thumb at me and I said for him,

"Yes, twenty-five thousand at interest to keep up the establishment."

"Yass. Den if Pastropbon go first to dat boneyard—" And out went his thumb again, while his hairy lip curled at the grim prospect of beating Fate the second time, and as badly, in the cemetery, as the first time, in the lottery.

He built the house—farther down town and much farther from the river. Both husband and wife found a daily delight in watching its slow rise and progress. In the room behind the shop he still plied his art and she her needle as they had done all their married life, with never an inroad upon

their accustomed hours except the calls of
the shop itself; but on every golden morning of that luxurious summer-land, for a
little while before the carpenters and plas-
terers arrived and dragged off their coats,
the pair spent a few moments wandering
through and about the building together,
she with her hen-like crooning, he with his
unsmiling face.

Yet they never showed the faintest desire
to see the end. The contractor dawdled by
the month. I never saw such dillydallying.
They only abetted it, and when once he
brought an absurd and unasked-for excuse
to the taxidermist's shop, its proprietor
said—first shutting the door between them
and the wife in the inner room:

"Tek yo' time. Mo' sloweh she grow,
mo' longeh she stan'."

I doubt that either Manouvrier or his wife
hinted to the other the true reason for their
apathy. But I guessed it, only too easily,
and felt its pang. It was that with the oc-
cupancy and care of the house must begin
the wife's absence from her old seat beside
her husband at his work.

Another thing troubled me. I did persuade him to put fittings into his cistern which fire-engines could use in case of emergency, but he would not insure the building.

" Naw! Luck bring me dat—I let luck take care of her."

" Ah! yass," chimed the wife, " yet still I think mebbee the good God tell luck where to bring her. I'm shoe he got fing-er in that pie."

" Ah-ha? Daz all right! If God want to burn his own fing-er——"

At length the house was finished and was beautiful within and without. It was of two and a half stories, broad and with many rooms. Two spacious halls crossed each other, and there were wide verandas front and back, and a finished and latticed basement. The basement and the entire grounds, except a few bright flower-borders, were flagged, as was also the sidewalk, with the manufactured stone which in that nearly frostless climate makes such a perfect and beautiful pavement, and on this fair surface fell the large shadows of laburnum, myrtle, orange, oleander, sweet-olive, mespelus, and banana, which the taxidermist had not spared expense to transplant here in the leafy prime of their full growth.

Then almost as slowly the dwelling was furnished. In this the brother-in-law's widow co-operated, and when it was completed Manouvrier suggested her living in it a few days so that his wife might herself move in as leisurely as she chose. And six months later, there, in the old back room in St. Peter Street, the wife still sat sewing and now and then saying small, wise, dispassionate things to temper the warmth of her partner's more artistic emotions. Every fair day, about the hour of sunset, they went to see the new house. It was plain they loved it; loved it only less than their old life; but only the brother-in-law's widow lived in it.

VII

I HAPPENED about this time to be acting as president of an insurance company on Canal Street. Summer was coming in again. One hot sunny day, when the wind was high and gusty, the secretary was remarking to me what sad ruin it might work if fire should start among the frame tenement cottages which made up so many neighborhoods that were destitute of water-mains, when right at our ear the gong sounded for just such a region and presently engine after engine came thundering and smoking by our open windows. Fire had broken out in the street where Manouvrier's new house stood, four squares from that house, but straight to windward of it.

We knew only too well, without being there to witness, that our firemen would find nothing with which to fight the flames except a few shallow wells of surface water and the wooden rain-water cisterns above ground, and that both these sources were almost worthless owing to a drouth. A

man came in and sat telling me of his new
device for lessening the risks of fire.

"Where?" asked I, quickly.

"Why, as I was saying, on steamboats
loaded with cotton."

"Oh, yes," said I, "I understand." But
I did not. For the life of me I couldn't
make sense of what he said. I kept my eyes
laboriously in his face, but all I could see
was a vision of burning cottages; hook-and-
ladder-men pulling down sheds and fences;
ruined cisterns letting just enough water
into door-yards and street-gutters to make
sloppy walking; fire-engines standing idle
and dropping cinders into their own pud-
dles in a kind of shame for their little worth;
here and there one furiously sucking at an
exhausted well while its firemen stood with
scorching faces holding the nozzles almost
in the flames and cursing the stream of
dribbling mud that fell short of their gallant
endeavor. I seemed to see streets populous
with the sensation-seeking crowd; side-
walks and alleys filled with bedding, chairs,
bureaus, baskets of crockery and calico
clothing with lamps spilling into them,

cheap looking-glasses unexpectedly answering your eye with the boldness of an outcast girl, broken tables, pictures of the Virgin, overturned stoves, and all the dear mantlepiece trash which but an hour before had been the pride of the toiling housewife, and the adornment of the laborer's home.

"Where can I see this apparatus?" I asked my patient interviewer.

"Well—ahem! it isn't what you'd call an apparatus, exactly. I have here——"

"Yes; never mind that just now; I'm satisfied you've got a good thing and—I'll tell you! Can you come in to-morrow at this hour? Good! I wish you would! Well, good-day."

The secretary was waiting to speak to me. The fire, he said, had entirely burned up one square and was half through a second. "By the way, isn't that the street where old P. T. B.——"

"Yes," I replied, taking my hat; "if anyone wants to see me, you'd better tell him to call to-morrow."

I found the shop in St. Peter's Street shut, and went on to the new residence. As I came near it, its beauty seemed to me to have consciously increased under the threatenings of destruction.

In the front gate stood the brother-in-law's widow, full of gestures and distressful smiles as she leaned out with nervously folded arms and looked up and down the street. " Manouvrier? he is ad the fire since a whole hour. He will break his heart if dat fire ketch to dat 'ouse here. He cannot know 'ow 'tis in danger! Ah! sen' him word? I sen' him fo' five time'—he sen' back I stay righd there an' not touch nut'n'! Ah! my God! I fine dat varrie te-de-ous, me, yass!"

" Is his wife with him?"

" Assuredly! You see, dey git 'fraid 'bout dat 'ouse of de Sister', you know?"

" No, where is it?"

" No? You dunno dat lill' 'ouse where de Sister' keep dose orphelin' ba-bee'—juz big-inning sinse 'bout two week' ago— round de corner—one square mo' down town—'alf square mo' nearer de swamp? Well, I thing 'f you pass yondeh you fine Pastropbon."

VIII

THROUGH smoke, under falling cinders, and by distracted and fleeing households I went. The moment I turned the second corner I espied the house. It was already half a square from the oncoming fire, but on the northern side of the street, just out of its probable track and not in great danger except from sparks. But it was old and roofed with shingles; a decrepit Creole cottage sitting under dense cedars in a tangle of rose and honeysuckle vines, and strangely beautified by a flood of smoke-dimmed yellow sunlight.

As I hurried forward, several men and boys came from the opposite direction at a run and an engine followed them, jouncing and tilting across the sidewalk opposite the little asylum, into a yard, to draw from a fresh well. Their leader was a sight that drew all eyes. He was coatless and hatless; his thin cotton shirt, with its sleeves rolled up to the elbows, was torn almost off his shaggy breast, his trousers were drenched with water and a rude bandage round his head was soaked with blood. He carried an axe. The throng shut him from my sight, but I ran to the spot and saw him again standing before the engine horses with his back close to their heads. A strong, high board fence shut them off from the well and against it stood the owner of the property, pale as death, guarding the precious water with a shotgun at full cock. I heard him say:

"The first fellow that touches this fence——"

But he did not finish. Quicker than his gun could flash and bang harmlessly in the air the man before him had dropped the axe and leaped upon him with the roar of a lion. The empty gun flew one way and its owner another and almost before either struck the ground the axe was swinging and crashing into the fence.

As presently the engine rolled through the gap and shouting men backed her to the edge of the well, the big axeman paused to wipe the streaming sweat from his begrimed face with his arm. I clutched him.

" Manouvrier! "

A smile of recognition shone for an instant and vanished as I added,

" Come to your own house! Come, you can't save it here."

He turned a quick, wild look at the fire, seized me by the arm and with a gaze of deepest gratitude, asked:

" You tryin' save her? "

" I'll do anything I can."

" Oh, dass right! " His face was full of mingled joy and pain. " You go yondeh —mek yo' possible! " We were hurrying to the street—" Oh, yass, faw God's sake go, mek yo' possible! "

" But, Manouvrier, you must come too! Where's your wife? The chief danger to your house isn't here, it's where the fire's between it and the wind! "

His answer was a look of anguish. " Good God! my fran'. We come yondeh so quick we can! But—foudre tonnerre!— look that house here fill' with ba-bee'! What we goin' do? Those Sister' can't climb on roof with bocket' wateh. You see I got half-dozen boy' up yondeh; if I go 'way they dis-cend and run off at the fire, spark' fall on roof an'—" his thumb flew out.

"Sparks! Heavens! Manouvrier, your house is in the path of the *flames!*"

The man flew at me and hung over me, his strong locks shaking, his great black fist uplifted and the only tears in his eyes I ever saw there. "Damnession! She's not mine! I trade her to God faw these one! Go! tell him she's his, he kin burn her if he feel like'!" He gave a half laugh, fresh witness of his distress, and went into the gate of the asylum.

I smiled—what could I do?—and was turning away, when I saw the chief of the fire department. It took but one moment to tell him my want, and in another he had put the cottage roof under the charge of four of his men with instructions not to leave it till the danger was past or the house burning. The engine near us had drawn the well dry and was coming away. He met it, pointed to where, beneath swirling billows of black smoke, the pretty gable of the taxidermist's house shone like a white sail against a thundercloud, gave orders and disappeared.

The street was filling with people. A row of cottages across the way was being emptied. The crackling flames were but half a square from Manouvrier's house. I called him once more to come. He waved his hand kindly to imply that he knew what I had done. He and his wife were in the Sisters' front garden walk conversing eagerly with the Mother Superior. They neared the gate. Suddenly the Mother Superior went back, the lay-sister guarding the gate let the pair out and the three of us hurried off together.

We found ourselves now in the uproar and vortex of the struggle. Only at intervals could we take our attention from the turmoil that impeded or threatened us, to glance forward at the white gable or back —as Manouvrier persisted in doing—to the Sisters' cottage. Once I looked behind and noticed, what I was loath to tell, that the firemen on its roof had grown busy; but as I was about to risk the truth, the husband and wife, glancing at their own roof, in one

86

breath groaned aloud. Its gleaming gable had begun to smoke.

"Ah! that good God have pity on uz!" cried the wife, in tears, but as she started to run forward I caught her arm and bade her look again. A strong, white stream of water was falling on the smoking spot and it smoked no more.

The next minute, with scores of others, choking and blinded with the smoke, we were flying from the fire. The wind had turned.

"It is only a gust," I cried, "it will swing round again. We must turn the next corner and reach the house from the far side." I glanced back to see why my companions lagged and lo! they had vanished.

IX

I REACHED the house just in time to save its front grounds from the invasion of the rabble. The wind had not turned back again. The brother-in-law's widow was offering prayers of thanksgiving. The cisterns were empty and the garden stood glistening in the afternoon sun like a May queen drenched in tears; but the lovely spot was saved.

I left its custodian at an upper window, looking out upon the fire, and started once more to find my friends. Half-way round to the Sisters' cottage I met them. With many others I stepped aside to make a clear way for the procession they headed. The sweet, clean wife bore in her arms an infant; the tattered, sooty, bloody-headed husband bore two; and after them, by pairs and hand in hand, with one gray sister in the rear, came a score or more of pink-frocked, motherless little girls. An amused rabble of children and lads hovered about the diminutive column, with leers and jests and happy antics, and the wife smiled foolishly and burned red with her embarrassment; but in the taxidermist's face shone an exaltation of soul greater than any I had ever seen. I felt too petty for such a moment and hoped he would go by without seeing me; but he smiled an altogether new smile and said,

"My fran', God A'mighty, he know a good bargain well as anybody!"

I ran ahead with no more shame of the crowd than Zaccheus of old. I threw open the gate, bounded up the steps and spread wide the door. In the hall, the widow, knowing naught of this, met me with wet eyes crying,

"Ah! ah! de 'ouse of de orphelin' is juz blaze' up h-all over h-at once!" and hushed in amazement as the procession entered the gate.

P. T. B. Manouvrier, Taxidermist!

When the fire was out the owner of that sign went back to his shop and to his work, and his wife sat by him sewing as before. But the orphans stayed in their new and

better home. Two or three years ago the
Sisters—the brother-in-law's widow is one
of them—built a large addition behind; but
the house itself stands in the beauty in
which it stood on that day of destruction,
and my friend always leaves his work on
balmy afternoons in time to go with his
wife and see that pink procession, four
times as long now as it was that day, march
out the gate and down the street for its
daily walk.

"Ah! Pastropbon, we got ba-bee' enough
presently, en't it?"

"Ole woman, nobody else ever strock dat
lott'ree for such a prize like dat."

The Entomologist

The Entomologist

I

AN odd feature of New Orleans is the way homes of all ranks, in so many sections of it, are mingled. The easy, bright democracy of the thing is what one might fancy of ancient Greeks; only, here there is a general wooden frailty.

A notable phase of this characteristic is the multitude of small, frame, ground-story double cottages fronting endwise to the street, on lots that give either side barely space enough for one row of twelve-foot rooms with windows on a three-foot alley leading to the narrow backyard.

Thus they lie, deployed in pairs or half-dozens, by hundreds, in the variable intervals that occur between houses and gardens of dignity and elegance; hot as ovens, taking their perpetual bath of the great cleanser, sunshine. Sometimes they open directly upon the banquette (sidewalk), but often behind as much as a fathom of front-yard, as gay with flowers as a girl's hat, and as fragrant of sweet-olive, citronelle, and heliotrope as her garments. In the right-hand half of such a one, far down on the Creole side of Canal street, and well out toward the swamp, lived our friend the entomologist.

Just a glance at it was enough to intoxicate one's fancy. It seemed to confess newness of life, joy, passion, temperance, refinement, aspiration, modest wisdom, and serene courage. You would say there must live two well-mated young lovers—but one can't always tell.

The Entomologist

II

WE first came to know the entomologist
through our opposite neighbors, the Fontenettes, when we lived in the street that
still bears the romantic name, Sixth. What
a pity nothing rhymes to it. *Their* ground-
story cottage was of a much better sort.
It lay broadside to the street, two-thirds
across a lot of forty feet width, in the good
old Creole fashion, its front garden twelve
feet deep, and its street fence, of white pal-
ings, higher than the passer's head. The
parlor and dining-room were on the left,
and the two main bedrooms on the right,
next the garden; Mrs. Fontenette's in front,
opening into the parlor, Monsieur's behind,
letting into the dining-room. For there had
been a broader garden on the parlor and
dining-room side, but that had been sold
and built on. I fancy that if Mrs. Fontenette—who was not a Creole, as her husband was, but had once been a Miss Bangs,
or something, and still called blackberries
" blackbries," and made root rhyme with

foot—I fancy if she had been doomed to our entomologist's sort of a house she would have been too broken in spirit to have made anybody's acquaintance.

For our pretty blonde neighbor had ambitions, or *had* had, as she once hinted to me with a dainty sadness. When I somehow let slip to her that I had repeated her delicately balanced words to my wife she gave me one melting glance of reproach, and thenceforth confided in me no more beyond the limits of literary criticism and theology—and botany. I remember we were among the few roses of her small flower-beds at the time, and I was trying to show her what was blighting them all in the bud. She called them " rose-es."

They rarely bloomed for her; she was always for being the rose herself—as Monsieur Fontenette once said; but he said it with a glance of fond admiration. Her name was Flora, and yet not flowers, but their book-lore, best suited her subtle capriciousness. She made such a point of names that she could not let us be happy with the homely monosyllable by which we

were known, until we allowed her to hy-
phenate us as the Thorndyke-Smiths.

There hung in our hall an entire un-
marred beard of the beautiful gray Spanish
moss, eight feet long. I had got this
unusual specimen by tiptoeing from the
thwarts of a skiff with twelve feet of yellow
crevasse-waters beneath, the shade of the
vast cypress forest above, and the bough
whence it hung brought within hand's reach
for the first time in a century. Thus I explained it one day to Mrs. Fontenette, as
she touched its ends with a delicate finger.

" Tillandsia "—was her one word of response. She loved no other part of botany
quite so much as its Latin.

" The Baron ought to see that," said
Monsieur. He was a man of quiet manners, not over-social, who had once enjoyed
a handsome business income, but had early
—about the time of his marriage—been
made poor through the partial collapse of
the house in Havre whose cotton-buyer he
had been, and, in a scant way, still was.
" When a cotton-buyer geds down, he
stays," was all the explanation he ever gave

us. He had unfretfully let adversity cage
him for life in the only occupation he knew,
while the wife he adored kept him pecuni-
arily bled to death, without sharing his
silent resigna— There I go again! Somehow I can't talk about her without seeming
unjust and rude. I felt it just now, even,
when I quoted her husband's fond word,
that she always chose to be the rose herself.
Well, she nearly always succeeded; she was
a rose—with some of the rose's drawbacks.

When we asked who the Baron might
be it was she who told us, but in a certain
disappointed way, as if she would rather
have kept him unknown a while longer. He
was, she said, a profoundly learned man,
graduate of one of those great universities
over in his native Germany, and a naturalist.
Young? Well, eh—comparatively—yes.
At which the silent husband smiled his
dissent.

The Baron was an entomologist. Both
the Fontenettes thought we should be fascinated with the beauty of some of his cases
of moths and butterflies.

"And coleoptera," said the soft rose-

wife. She could ask him to bring them to us. Take us to him?—Oh!—eh—her embarrassment made her prettier, as she broke it to us gently that the Baroness was a seamstress. She hushed at her husband's mention of shirts; but recovered when he harked back to the Baron, and beamed her unspoken apologies for the great, brave scholar who daily, silently bore up under this awful humiliation.

III

TOWARD the close of the next afternoon she brought the entomologist. I can see yet the glad flutter she could not hide as they came up our front garden walk in an air spiced by the "four-o'clocks," with whose small trumpets—red, white, and yellow—our children were filling their laps and stringing them on the seed-stalks of the cocoa-grass. He was bent and spectacled, of course; *l'entomologie oblige;* but, oh, besides!—

"Comparatively young," Mrs. Fontenette

had said, and I naturally used her husband, who was thirty-one, for the comparison. Why, this man? It would have been a laughable flattery to have guessed his age to be forty-five. Yet that was really the fact. Many a man looks younger at sixty —oh, at sixty-five! He was dark, bloodless, bowed, thin, weatherbeaten, ill-clad—a picture of decent, incurable penury. The best thing about his was his head. It was not imposing at all, but it was interesting, albeit very meagrely graced with fine brown hair, dry and neglected. I read him through without an effort before we had been ten minutes together; a leaf still hanging to humanity's tree, but faded and shrivelled around some small worm that was feeding on its juices.

And there was no mistaking that worm; it was the avarice of knowledge. He had lost life by making knowledge its ultimate end, and was still delving on, with never a laugh and never a cheer, feeding his emaciated heart on the locusts and wild honey of entomology and botany, satisfied with them for their own sake, without reference to God or man; an infant in emotions, who time and again would no doubt have starved outright but for his wife, whom there and then I resolved we should know also. I was amused to see, by stolen glances, Mrs. Smith study him. She did not know she frowned, nor did he; but Mrs. Fontenette knew it every time.

We all had the advantage of him as to common sight. His glasses were obviously of a very high power, yet he could scarcely see anything till he clapped his face close down and hunted for it. When he pencilled for me the new Latin name he had given to a small, slender, almost dazzling green beetle inhabiting the Spanish moss—his own scientific discovery—he wrote it so minutely that I had to use a lens to read it.

As we sat close around the library lamp, I noticed how often his poor clothing had been mended by a woman's needle. His linen was discouraging, his cravat awry and dingy, and his hands—we had better pass his hands; yet they were slender and refined.

Also they shook, though not from any habit commonly called vicious. You could see that no vice of the body nor any lust of material things had ever led him captive. He gave one the tender despair with which we look on a blind babe.

When we expressed regret that his wife had not come with him, he only bent with a deeper greed into a book I had handed him, and after a moment laid it down disappointedly, saying that it was "fool of plundters." Mrs. Fontenette asking to be shown one of them, they reopened the book together, she all consciousness as she bent against him over the page, he oblivious of everything but the phrase they were hunting. He gave his forehead a tap of despair as he showed where the book called this same Tillandsia, or Spanish moss, a parasite.

"It iss no baraseet," he explained, in a mellow falsetto, "it iss an epipheet!"

"An air-plant!" said his fair worshipper, softly drinking in a bosomful of gladness as she made the distance between them more discreet.

Distances were all one to him. He seemed like a burnt log, still in shape but gone to ashes, except in one warm spot where glowed this self-consuming, world-sacrificing adoration of knowledge; knowledge sought, as I say, purely for its own sake and narrowed down to names and technical descriptions. Men of *perverted* principles and passions you may find anywhere; but I never had seen anyone so totally undeveloped in all the emotions, affections, tastes that make life *life*.

IV

A FEW afternoons later I went to his house. For pretext I carried a huge green worm, but I went mainly to see just how unluckily he was married. He was not at home. I found his partner a small, bright, toil-worn, pretty woman of hardly twenty-eight or nine, whose two or three children had died in infancy, and who had blended wifehood and motherhood together, and was taking care of the Baron as a widow would care for a crippled son, and at the same time reverencing him as if he were a demigod. Of his utter failure to provide their daily living she confessed herself by every implication, simply—proud! What else should a demigod's wife expect? At the same time, without any direct statement, she made it clear that she had no disdain, but only the broadest charity, for men who make a living. It was odd how few her smiles were, and droll how much sweetness —what a sane winsomeness—she managed to radiate without them. I left her in her clean, bright cottage, like a nesting bird in a flowery bush, and entered my own home, declaring, with what I was gently told was unnecessary enthusiasm, that the Baron's wife was the "unluckily married" one, and the best piece of luck her husband had ever had. I had seen women make a virtue of necessity, but I had never before seen one make a conviction, comfort, and joy of it, and I should try to like the Baron, I said, if only for her sake.

Of course I became, in some degree, a source of revenue to him. Understand, there was always a genuine exchange of so much for so much; he was not a "baraseet" —oh, no!—yet he hung on. We still have,

stowed somewhere, a large case of butterflies, another of splendid moths, and a
smaller one of glistening beetles. Nor can
I begrudge their cost, of whatever sort, even
now when my delight in them is no longer
a constant enthusiasm. The cases of specimens have passed from daily sight, but
thenceforth, as never before, our garden was
furnished with guests—pages, ladies, poets,
fairies, emperors, goddesses—coming and
going on gorgeous wings, and none ever a
stranger more than once. My non-para-
sitic friend " opened a new world " to me;
a world that so flattered one with its grace
and beauty, its marvellous delicacy and
minuteness, its glory of color and curious-
ness of marking, and its exquisite adapta-
tion of form to need and function, that in
my meaner depths, or say my childish shal-
lows—I resented Mrs. Fontenette's making
the same avowal for herself—I didn't believe her!

I do not say she was consciously sham-
ming; but I could see she drank in the
Baron's revelations with no more true spiritual exaltation than the quivering twilight

moths drew from our veranda honeysuckles.
Yet it was mainly her vanity that feasted,
not any lower impulse—of which, you
know, there are several—and, possibly, all
her vanity craved at first was the tinsel dis-
tinction of unusual knowledge.

One night she got into my dreams. I
seemed to be explaining to Monsieur Fontenette apologetically that this newly opened
world was not at all separate from my old
one, but shone everywhere in it, like our
winged guests in our garden, and followed
and surrounded me far beyond the Baron's
company, terminology, and magnifying-
glass, lightening the burdens and stress of
the very counting-room and exchange.
Whereat he seemed to flare up!

"Ah!—you—I believe yes! But she?"
he waved his hand in fierce unbelief.

I awoke concerned, and got myself to
sleep again only by remembering the utter
absence of vanity in the Baron himself. I
lay smiling in the dark to think how much
less all our verbal caressings were worth to
him than the drone of the most familiar
beetle, and how his life-long delving in

The Entomologist

books and nature had opened up this fairy world to him only at the cost of shutting up all others. If education means calling forth and perfecting our powers and affections, he was ten times more uneducated than his wife, even as we knew her then. He appeared to care no more for human interests, far or near, in large or small, than a crab cares for the stars. I fell asleep chuckling in remembrance of an occasion when Mrs. Fontenette, taking her cue from me, spoke to him of his plant-and-insect lore as one of the many worlds there are within *the* world, no more displacing it than light displaces air, or than fragrance displaces form or sound. He made her say it all over again, and then asked: " Vhere vas dat? "

His whole world was not really as wide as Gregory's island was to its gentle hermit. No butterfly raptures for him; he devoured the one kind of facts he cared for, as a caterpillar devours leaves.

V

How Mrs. Fontenette got Mrs. " Thorn-
dyke-Smith " and me entangled with some
six or eight others in her project for a
botanizing and butterfly-chasing picnic I do
not know; but she did. On the evening
before the appointed day I perfidiously
crawfished out of it, and our house furnished only one delegate, whom I urged to
go rather than break up the party—I never
break up a party if I can avoid it. " But as
for me going," I said, " my business simply
won't let me! " At which our pretty neighbor expressed her regrets with a ready
resignation that broke into open sunshine
as she lamented the same inability in her
husband. To my suggestion that the
Baroness be invited, Mrs. Fontenette smiled
a sweet amusement that was perfect in its
way, and said she hoped the weather would
be propitious; people were so timid about
rain.

It was. When I came home, tardily, that
afternoon, the picnickers had not returned,

though the oleanders and crape-myrtles on
the grounds next ours cast shadows three
times their length across our lawn. In an
aimless way I roamed from the house down
into our small rear garden, thinking oftenest, of course, of the absentees, and admiring the refined good sense with which Monsieur Fontenette seemed to have decided to
let this unperilous attack of silliness run itself out in the woman he loved with so much
tenderness and with so much passion.

"How much distress he is saving himself and all of us," I caught myself mur-
muring, audibly, out among my fig-trees.

Finding two or three figs fully ripe, I
strolled over the way to see him among his
trees and maybe find chance for a little
neighborly boasting. As our custom with
each other was, I ignored the bell on his
gate, drew the bolt, and, passing in among
Mrs. Fontenette's invalid roses, must have
moved, without intention, quite noiselessly
from one to another, until I came around
behind the house, where a strong old cloth-
of-gold rose-vine half covered the latticed
side of the cistern shed. In the doorway I

stopped in silent amaze. A small looking-glass hanging against the wooden cistern showed me—although I was in much the stronger light—Monsieur Fontenette. He was just straightening up from an oil-stone he had been using, and the reflection of his face fell full on the glass. Once before, but once only, had I seen such agony of countenance—such fierce and awful looking in and out at the same time; that was on a man who was still trying to get the best of a fight in which he knew he was mortally shot. Fontenette did not see me. I suppose the rose-vine screened me, and his glance did not rise quite to the mirror, but followed the soft thumbings with which he tried the two edges and point of as murderous a knife as ever I saw.

As softly as a shadow I drew out of sight, turned away, and went almost back to the gate before I let my footfall be heard, and called, " M'sieu' Fontenette! "

He hallooed from the shed in a playful sham of being a mile or so away, and emerged from the lattice and vine with that accustomed light of equanimity on his feat-

ures which made him always so thoroughly
good-looking. He came hitching his waist-
band with both hands in that innocent
Creole way that belongs to the latitude, and
how I knew I cannot tell you, but I did
know—I didn't merely feel or think, but I
knew!—*positively*—that he had that hideous
thing on his person.

Against what contingency I could only
ask myself and wonder, but I instantly decided to get him away from home and keep
him away until the picnickers had got back
and scattered. So I proposed a walk, a diversion we had often enjoyed together.

" Yes? " he said, " to pazz the time whilse
they don't arrive? With the greates' of
pleasu'e! "

I dare say we were both more preoccu-
pied than we thought we were, for outside
the gate we fairly ran into a lady—yes; a
seamstress—the wife of the entomologist.
My stars! She had seemed winning enough
before, but now—what a rise in values! As
we conversed it was all I could do to keep
my eyes from saying: " A man with you for
a wife belongs at home whenever he can

be there!'' But whether they spoke it or not, in some way, without word or glance, by simple radiations from the whole sweet woman, she revealed that to make that fact plain to him, to *her*, and to all of us, was what this new emphasis of charm was for.

She had come, she said—and scarcely on the lips of the loveliest Creole did I ever hear a more bewitching broken-English— she had come according to a half-promise made to Mrs. Fontenette to show her—" I tidn't etsectly promised, I chust said I vill some time come——"

"And Mrs. Fontenette didn't object," I playfully interrupted—

"No," said the unruffled speaker, "I chust said I vill come; yes; to show her a new vay to remoof, remoof? is sat English? So? A new vay to remoof old stains."

"A new way—" responded Fontenette, with an air of gravest interest in all matters of laundry.

"Yes," she repeated, as simply as a babe, "a new vay; and I sought I come now so to go home viss mine hussbandt." There, at last, she smiled, and to make the caress-

ing pride of her closing tone still prettier,
lifted her figured muslin out sidewise between thumb and forefinger of each hand
with even more archaic grace than playfulness.

As the three of us crossed over and took
seats on my veranda, we were joined by
the neighbor whose garden-trees I have
mentioned; the man of whom I have told
you, how he failed to strike a bargain with
old Manouvrier, the taxidermist. He was
a Missourian, in the produce business, a
thoroughly good fellow, but—well—oh—!

He came perspiring, flourishing a palm-
leaf fan and a large handkerchief, to say
I might keep all the shade his tall house
and trees dropped on my side of the fence.
And presently what does the simple fellow
do but begin to chaff the three of us on the
absence of our three partners!

VI

I HELD my breath in dismay! The more I strove to change the subject the more our fat wag, fancying he was teasing me to the delight of the others, harped on the one string, until with pure apprehension of what Fontenette might presently do or say, my blood ran hot and cold. But Monsieur showed neither amusement nor annoyance, only a perfectly gracious endurance. Yet how could I know what instant his forbearance might give way, or what serpent's eggs the joker's inanities might in the next day or hour turn out to be, laid in the hot heart of the Creole gentleman? Then it was that this slender little German seamstress-wife shone forth like the first star of the breathless twilight.

Seamstress? no; she had left the seamstress totally behind her. You might have thought the finest tactics of the drawing-room—not of to-day, but of the times when gentlemen wore swords and dirks—had been at her finger-ends all her life. She

The Entomologist

took our good neighbor's giddy pleasant-
ries as deep truths lightly put, and answered
them in such graceful, mild earnest, and
with such a modest, yet fetching, quaint-
ness, that we were all preached to more
effectively than we could have been by seven
priests from one pulpit. Or, at any rate,
that was my feeling; every note she uttered
was melodiously kind, but every sentence
was an arrow sent home.

"You make me," she said, "you make
me sink of se aunt of my musser, vhat she
said to my musser vhen my musser iss getting married. 'Senda,' she said, 'vonce in
a vhile'—is sat right, 'vonce in a vhile?'—
so?—'vonce in a vhile your Rudolph going
to see a voman he better had married san
you. Sen he going to fall a little vay—
maybe a good vay—in love viss her; and
sen if Rudolph iss a scoundtrel, or if you iss
a fool, sare be trouble. But if Rudolph
don't be a scoundtrel and you don't be a
fool he vill pretty soon straight' up himself
and say, One man can't ever'sing have, and
mine Senda she is enough!' . . . Sat
vas my Aunt Senda."

"Your mother was named for her?"

"Yes, my musser, and me; I am name'
Senda, se same. She vas se Countess von
(Something)—sat aunt of my musser. She
vas a fine voman."

"Still," said our joker, "you know she
was only about half right in that advice."

"No," she replied, putting on a drowsy
tone, "I don't know; and I sink you don't
know eeser."

"I reckon I do," he insisted. "We're
all made of inflammable stuff. Any *man*
knows that. We couldn't, any of us, pull
through life decently if we didn't let each
other be each other's keeper; could we,
Fontenette?"

No sound from Fontenette. "Hmm!"
hummed the little woman, in such soft de-
rision that only he and I heard it; and after
a moment she said, "Yes, it is so. But,
you know who is se only good keeper? Sat
is love."

"And jealousy," suggested Bulk; "the
blindfold boy and the green-eyed monster."

"Se creen-eyedt—no, I sink not. Chalousie have destroyed—is sat correct?—

yes? Chalousie have destroyed a sowsand-
sowsand times so much happiness as it ever
saved—ah! see se lightening! I sink sat
is se displeasu'e of heaven to my so bad
English. Ah? see it again? Vell, I vill
stop."

"You ought to be in a better world than
this," laughed our fat neighbor.

"No," she chanted, "I rasser sis one. I
sink mine hussbandt never be satisfied viss
a vorld not full of vorms and bugs; and I
am glad to stay alvays viss mine hussbandt."

"And I reckon he thinks you're big
enough world for him, just yourself, doesn't
he?"

"No." She seemed to speak more than
half to herself. "A man—see se lightening!—a man who can be satisfied viss a
vorld no bigger as I can by mineself gif
him—mine Kott! I vould not haf such a
man! See se lightening! but I sink sare
vill be no storm; sare is no sunder viss se
ligh'—Ah! sare are se trhuants!" We rose
to meet them. First came the children,
vaunting their fatigue, then a black maid or

two, with twice their share of baskets, and
then our three spouses; the Baron came last
and was mute. The two ladies called cheery,
weary good-byes to another contingent,
that passed on by the gate, and hail and
farewell to our fat neighbor as he went
home. Then they yielded their small burdens to us, climbed the veranda stairs and
entered the house.

VII

No battle, it is said, is ever fought, and
I dare say no game—worth counting—is
ever played, exactly as previously planned.
One of our company had planned, very
secretly, as he thought, a battle; another,
almost openly, was already waging hers;
while a third was playing a game—though
probably, I admit, fighting, inwardly, her
poor weak battle also; and none of the
three offered an exception to this rule. The
first clear proof of it—which it still gives
me a low sort of pleasure to recall—was my
prompt discovery, as we gathered around
the tea-board, to eat the picnic's remains,

The Entomologist

that our Flora was out of humor with the
Baron. It was plain that the whole day's
flood of small experiences had been to her
pretty vanity a Tantalus's cup. She was
quick to tell, with an irritation, which she
genuinely tried to conceal, and with scarcely an ounce of words to a ton of dead-sweet
insinuation, what a social failure he had
chosen to be. Evidently he had spent every
golden hour of sweet spiritual opportunity
—I speak from her point of view, or, at least,
my notion of it—not in catching and com-
municating the charm of any scene or inci-
dent, nor in thrilling comparisons of senti-
ment with anyone, nor in any impartation
of inspiring knowledge, nor in any mirthful
exchange of compliments or gay glances
over the salad and sandwiches; but in constantly poking and plodding through thicket
and mire and solitarily peering and prying
on the under sides of leaves and stems and
up and down and all around the bark of
every rough-trunked tree.

She made the picture amusing, none the
less, and to no one more so than to the
Baron's wife, whose presence among us at

the board was as fragrant, so to speak, as that of a violet among its leaves and sisters. "Ah! Gustaf," she said, with a cadenced gravity more taking than mirth, " sat iss a treat-ment nobody got a right to but me. But tell me, tell se company, vhat new sings have you found? I know you have not hunt' all se day and nussing new found."

But the Baron had found nothing new. He told us so with his mouth dripping and his nose in the trough—his plate I should say. You could hear him chew across the room. Suddenly, however, he ceased eating and began to pour forth an account of his day's observation; in response to which M. Fontenette, to my amused mystification, led us all in the interest with which we listened. The Baron forgot his food, and when reminded of it, pushed it away with a grunt and talked on and on, while we almost forgot our own.

As we rose to return to the veranda, the Creole still offered him an undivided attention, which the Baron rewarded with his continued discourse. As I gave Fontenette a light for his cigarette I held his eye for a

The Entomologist

moment with a brightness of face into which
I put as significant approval as I dared; for
I fancied the same unuttered word was
brooding in both our hearts: " A new vay
to remoof old stains."

Then he turned and gave all his attention
once more to the entomologist, as they
walked out upon the gallery together behind their wives. And the German woman
courted the pretty New Englander as sweetly as the Creole courted her husband, and
with twice the energy. She was a bubbling
spring of information in the Baron's science;
she was a well of sweet philosophy on life
and conduct, and at every turn of their con-
versation, always letting Mrs. Fontenette
turn it, she showed her own to be the better
mind and the better training.

When Mrs. Fontenette, before any one
else, rose to go—maybe my dislike of her
only made it seem so—but I believed she
did it out of pure bafflement and chagrin.

Not so believed her husband. He responded gratefully; yet lingered, still listening to the entomologist, until she fondlingly
chid him for forgetting that while he had

been all day in his swivel-chair, she had passed the hours in unusual fatigues!

She declined his arm in our garden walk, and positively forbade me to cut a rose for her—but with a grace almost maidenly. As I let them out, the heat-lightning gleamed again low in the west. A playfulness came into M. Fontenette's face and he murmured to me, " See se lightening."

" Yes," I replied, pressing his hand, " but I sink sare vill be no storm if sare iss no sunder."

Mrs. Fontenette gave a faint gasp of impatience and left us at a run, tripping fairily across the rough street at the only point visible to those on the veranda. Fontenette scowled unaware as he started to follow, and the next moment a short " aha! " escaped him. For, at her gate, to my unholy joy, she stumbled just enough to make the whole performance unspeakably ridiculous, and flirted into her cottage——

" In tears! " I offered to bet myself as I turned to rejoin my companions on the veranda, and wished with all my soul the goggled Baron could have seen it.

The Entomologist

VIII

BUT the best of eyes would not have counted this time, for he was not there. He had accepted the offer of a room, where he was giving the day's specimens certain treatments which he believed, or pretended, could not wait until he should reach his far downtown cottage. His hostess and his wife had gone with him, but now some light discussion of house adornment was drawing them to the parlor. As this room was being lighted I saw our guest, evidently through force of an early habit, turn a critical glance to the music on the piano, and as quickly withdraw it. Both of us motioned her solicitously to the music-stool.

" No, I do not play."

" Then you sing."

" No, not now, any more yet." But when she had let us tease her a wee bit just for one little German song, she went to the instrument, talking slowly as she went, and closing the door in the entomologist's direction as she talked.

"Siss a great vhile I haf not done siss," she concluded, as her fingers began to drift over the keys, and then she sang, very gently, even guardedly, but oh, so sweetly!

We were amazed. Here, without the slightest splendor of achievement or adventure, seemed to be the most incredible piece of real life we had ever seen. Why, I asked myself, was this woman so short even of German friends as to be condemned to a seamstress's penury? And my best guess was to lay it to the zeal of her old-fashioned—and yet not merely old-fashioned—wifehood, which could accept no friendship that did not unqualifiedly accept him; and he?—Goodness!

When she ceased neither listener spoke; the tears were in our throats. She bent her head slightly over the keys, and said, "I like to sing you anusser." We accepted eagerly, and she sang again. There was nothing of personal application in either song, yet now, near the end, where there was a purposed silence in the melody, the silence hung on and on until it was clear she was struggling with herself; but again the strain arose without a tremor, and so she finished. " Oh, no, no," she replied, to our solicitation, with the grateful emphasis of one who declines a third glass, "se sooneh I stop, se betteh for ever'body," meaning specially herself, I fancy, speaking, as she rose, in a tone of such happy decision, and yet so melodiously, that two or three strings in the piano replied.

Her hostess took her hands and said there was one thing she could and must do; she and her husband must spend the night with us. There was a bed-chamber connected with the room where the Baron was still at work, and, really—this and that, and that and this—until in the heat of argument they called each other " My dear," and presently the ayes had it. The last word I heard from our fair guest was to her hostess at the door of her chamber, the farthest down the hall. It was as to shutting or not shutting the windows. " No," she said, " I sink sare vill be no storm, because sare is yet no sunder vis se lightening." And so it turned out. But at the same time——

IX

My room adjoined the Baron's in front as his wife's did farther back. A door of his and window of mine stood wide open on the one balcony, from which a flight of narrow steps led down into the side garden. Thus, for some time after I was in bed I heard him stirring; but by and by, with no sound to betoken it except the shutting of this door, it was plain he had lain down.

I awoke with a sense of having been some hours asleep, and in fact the full moon, shining gloriously, had passed the meridian. The balcony was lighted up by it like noon, and on it stood the entomologist, entirely dressed. The door was shut behind him. He was looking in at my window, but he did not know the room was mine, and with eyes twice as good as he had he could not have seen through my mosquito-bar. I wondered, but lay still till he had started softly down the steps. Then I sprang out of bed on the dark side, and dressed faster than a fireman.

The Entomologist

When half-clad I went and looked out a parlor window. He was trying the gate, which was locked. But he knew where the key always hung, behind the post, and turned to get it. I went back and finished dressing, stole down the inner, basement stairs and out into the deep shadows of the garden, and presently saw my guest passing in through the Fontenettes' gate, whose bolt he had drawn from the outside. As angry now as I had been amazed I hurried after.

To avoid the moonlight I followed the shadows of the sidewalk-trees down to the next corner, to cross there and come back under a like cover on the other side. But squarely on the crossing I was met and stopped by a belated drunkard, who had a proposition to make to me which he thought no true gentleman, such as he was, for instance, could decline. I was alone, he asked me to notice; and he was alone; but if he should go with me, which he would be glad to do, why, then, you see, we should be together. He stuck like a bur, and it was minutes before I got him well started off in

his own right direction. I slipped to the
Fontenettes' gate, as near as was best, and
instantly saw, between one of its posts and
a very black myrtle-orange, Fontenette himself, standing as still as the trees. I was
not in so deep a shade as he, but I might
have stepped right out into the moonlight
without his seeing me, so intensely was he
watching his wife's front door. For there
stood the entomologist. He had evidently
been knocking, and was about to knock
again when there came some response from
within, to which he replied, in a suppressed
yet eager and agitated voice, " Mine Psyche!
Oh, mine Psyche! She is come to me undt
she is bringing me already more as a hoon-
dredt—vhat? " He had been interrupted
from within. " Vhat you say? "

Fontenette drew his knife.

I stood ready to spring the instant he
should stir to advance. I realized almost
unbearably my position, stealing thus at
such a moment on the heels of my neighbor and friend, but this is not a story of
feelings, at any rate, not of mine.

" Vhat? " said the entomologist. " Go

avay? Mien Gott! No, I vill not ko avay.
Mien gloryform! Gif me first mine gloryform! Dot Psyche hass come out fon ter
grysalis! she hass drawn me dot room full
mit oder Psyches, undt you haf mine pottle
of gloryform in your pocket yet! Yes, ko
kit ut; I vait; ach!" Presently he seemed
to hear from inside a second approach.
Then the door opened an inch or so, and
with another "Ach!" and never a word of
thanks, he snatched the vial and, turning to
make off with it, came nose to nose with M.
Fontenette, who stood in the moonlight
gateway holding a blazing match to his
cigarette.

"Well, sir, good-evening again," said the
Creole. I noticed the perfection of his dress;
evidently he had not as yet loosed as much
as a shoestring. And then I observed also
that the visitor so close before him was without his shoes.

"Good-evening—or, good-morning, per-
chance," said Fontenette. "I suepose thaz
a great thing to remove those old stain' that
chloro*form*, eh?"

"Ach! it iss you? Ach, you must coom

—coom undt hellup me! Coom! you shall see *someding*."

"A moment," said the Creole. "May I inquire you how is that, that you call on us in yo' sock feet?"

"Ach! I am already t'e socks putting on pefore I remember I do not need t'em! But coom! coom! see a vonderfool!" He led, and Fontenette, when he had blown a cloud of smoke through his nose, followed, saying exclusively for his own ear:

"A wonder fool, yes! But a fool is no wonder to me any more; I find myself to be that kind."

X

WHEN, hypocritically clad in dressing-gown and slippers, I stopped at my guest's inner door and Fontenette opened it just enough to let me enter, I saw, indeed, a wonderful sight. The entomologist had lighted up the room, and it was filled, filled! with gorgeous moths as large as my hand and all of a kind, dancing across one another's airy paths in a bewildering maze or alight-

The Entomologist

ing and quivering on this thing and that.
The mosquito-net, draping almost from
ceiling to floor, was beflowered with them
majestically displaying in splendid alterna-
tion their upper and under colors, or, with
wings lifted and vibrant, tipping to one side
and another as they crept up the white mesh,
like painted and gilded sails in a fairies'
regatta.

And all this life and beauty, this gay glory
and tremorous ecstasy and effort was here
for moth-love of one incarnate fever of frail-
winged loveliness! Oh! to what unguessed
archangelic observation, to what infinite se-
raphic compassion, may not our own
swarming race, who dare not too much pity
ourselves, be but just such dainty ephem-
era! Splendid in purposes, intelligence,
and affections as these in colors and grace,
glorious when on the wing, and marvellous
still, riddles of wonder, even when crawling
and quivering, tipping and swerving from
the upright and true, like these palpitating
flowers of desire, now this way and now
that, forever drawn and driven by the sweet
tyrannies of instinct and impulse.

Strong Hearts

So rushed the thought in upon me, and if it was not of the divinest or manliest inspiration, at least it took some uncharity out of me for the moment. As in mechanical silence Fontenette obeyed the busy requests of the entomologist, I presently looked more on those two than on the winged multitude, and thought on, of the myriad true tales of love-weakness and love-wrath for which they and their two pretty mates were just now so unlucky as to stand; of the awful naturalness of such things; of the butterfly beauty and wonder—nay, rather the divine possibilities of the lives such things so naturally speed to wreck; and then of Tom Moore almost too playfully singing:

> Ah! did we take for Heaven above
>   But half such pains as we
> Take, day and night, for woman's love,
>   What Angels we should be!

But while I moralized there came a change. Beneath the entomologist's dark hand, as it searched and hurried throughout the room, the flutter of wings had ceased as under a wind of death.

The Entomologist

" You must have a hundred and fifty of them," I said as the last victim ceased to flutter.

" Yes."

" Their sale is slow, of course, but every time you sell one, you ought to get "—I was judging by some prices he had charged me—" you ought to get two dollars." And I secretly rejoiced for Senda.

" I not can afford to sell t'em," he replied, with his back to me.

" Why, how so? "

" No, it iss t'is kind vhat I can exshange for five, six, maybe seven specimenss fon Ahfrica undt Owstrahlia. No, I vill not sell t'em."

" Oh, I see," said I, in mortal disgust. " Fontenette, I'm going to bed." And Fontenette went too.

The next day was cloudless—in two hearts; Senda's, and Fontenette's. As to the sky, that is another matter; one of the charms of that warm wet land is that, with all its sunshine, it is almost never without clouds. And indeed it would be truer to say of my two friends' skies, that they had clouds, but the clouds were silvered through with happy reassurances. Jealousy, we are told, once set on fire, burns without fuel; but I must think that that is oftenest, if not always, the jealousy of a selfish love. Or, rather—let me quote Senda, as she spoke the only other time she ever touched upon the subject with us. Our fat neighbor had dragged it in again as innocently as a young dog brings an old shoe into the parlor, and, the Fontenettes being absent, she had the nerve and wisdom not to avoid it. Said she:

" Some of us—not all—have great power to love. Some, not all, who have sis power —to love—have also se power to trust. Me, I rasser be trustet and not loved, san to be loved and not trustet."

" How about a little of each? " asked our neighbor.

" Oh! If se *nature* iss little, sat iss, may-be, very vell—? " She spoke as kindly as a mother to her babe, but he stole a slow glance here and there, as though some one had shot him with a pea in church, and dropped the theme.

Which I, too, will do when I have noted

134

the one thing I had particularly in mind to say, of Fontenette: that, as Senda remarked —for the above is an abridgment—" I rasser see chalousie vissout cause, san cause vissout chalousie;" and that even while I was witness of the profound ferocity of his jealousy when roused, and more and more as time passed on, I was impressed with its sweet reasonableness.

XI

Time did pass—in days and weeks of that quiet sort which make us forget in actual life that such is the way in good stories also. Innumerable crops were growing in the fields, countless ships were sailing or steaming the monotonous leagues of their long wanderings from port to port, some empty, some heavy-laden, like bees between garden and hive:

The corn-tops were ripe and the meadows were in bloom
And the birds made music all the day.

Many of our days must not be the wine, but only small bits of the vine, of life. We

135

cannot gather or eat *them;* we can only let them grow, branch, blossom, get here and there green grapes, scarce a tenth of a tithe, in bulk or weight, of the whole growth, and " in due season—if we faint not " pluck the purpled clusters. And as the vine is—much, too, as the vine is tended, so will be the raisins and the wine. There is nothing in life for which to be more thankful, or in which to be more diligent, than its inter-missions. This is not my sermonizing. I am not going to put everything off upon " Senda," but really this was hers. I have edited it a trifle; her inability to make, in her pronunciation, a due difference between wine and vine rather dulled the point of her moral.

Fontenette remarked to her one Sunday afternoon in our garden, that she must have got her English first from books.

" Yes," she said, " I didt. Also I have many, many veeks English conversations lessons befo'e Ame'ica. But I cannot se p'onunciation get; because se spelling. Hah! I can *not* sat spelling get! "

The Entomologist

O, but didn't I want to offer my services? But, like Bunyan's Christian, I recalled a text and so got by; which text was the wise saying of that female Solomon, " se aunt of my muss-er "—" One man can't ever'sing have, and mine "—establishment is already complete.

Meantime, Mrs. Fontenette, from farthest off in our group, had slipped around to the Baroness. She spoke something low, stroking her downy fan and blushing with that damsel sweetness of which her husband was so openly fond.

" O no, I sank you! " answered Senda, in an undulating voice. " I sank you v'ey much, but I cannot take se time to come to yo' house, and I cannot let you take se trouble *too* come *too* mine. No, if I can have me only se right soughts, and find me se right vords for se right soughts, I sink I leave se p'onunciation to se mercy of P'ovidence."

Mrs. Fontenette blushed as prettily as a child, and let her husband take her hand as he said, " The Providence that wou'n' have mercy on such a pronunshation like

that—ah well, 'twould have to become v'ey
un'popular!"

"Anyhow," cooed Senda, "I risk it;"
and then to his wife—"For se present, siss
betteh I sew for you san spell for you."

Thus was our fair neighbor at every turn
overmatched by the trustful love of the man
and watchful love of the woman, whose fancied inferiority was her excuse for an illicit
infatuation; an infatuation which little by
little became a staring fact—only not to
Fontenette. You know, you can hide such
a thing from those who love and trust you,
but not long from those who do not; and
if you are not old in sin—Flora and the
Baron were infants—you will almost certainly think that a condition hid from those
who love and trust you is hid from all! O
fools! the very urchins of the playground
will presently have found you out and be
guessing at broken laws, though there be
only broken faiths and the anguish of first
steps in perfidy.

We could not help but see, and yet for
all our seeing we could not help. The matter never took on flagrancy enough to give

ever so kind an intervener a chance to speak
with effect. It was pitiful to see how little
gratification they got out of it; especially
she, with that silly belief in her ability to
rekindle his spiritual energies and lift him
into the thin air of her transcendentalisms;
slipping, nevertheless, bit by bit, down the
precipitous incline between her vaporous
refinements and his wallowing animalisms;
too destitute of the love that loves to give,
or of courage, or of cunning, to venture into
the fires of real passion, but forever craving
flattery and caresses, and for their sake forever holding him over the burning coals of
unfulfilled desire.

How could we know these things so
positively?

By the entomologist; the child of science.
Science yearns ever to know and to tell.
Truth for truth's sake! He had no strong
moral feeling against a lie; but he had never
had the slightest *use* for a lie, and a prevari-
cation on his tongue would have been as
strange to him as castanets in his palms.
Guile takes alertness, adroitness; and the
slim pennyworth of these that he could com-

mand he used up, no doubt, on Fontenette. I noticed that after an hour with the Creole he always looked tortured and exhausted. With us he was artless to the tips of his awful finger-nails.

Nor was Mrs. Fontenette a skilful dissembler; she over-concealed things so revealingly. Then she was so helplessly enamoured and in so childish a way. I venture one of the penalties almost any woman may have to pay for bringing to the altar only the consent to be loved is to find herself, some time, at last, far from the altar, a Titania, a love's fool. Our Titania pointed us to the fact that the Baron's wife never tried to divert his mind from the one pursuit that enthralled it; and she borrowed one of our garden alleys in which to teach him—grace-hoops! He never caught one from her nor threw one that she could catch; but, ah! with her coaxing and commanding, her sweet taunting and reprimanding and his utter lack of surprise at them, how much she betrayed! Fontenette came, learned in a few throws, and was charmed with the toys—a genuine lover always takes to them

The Entomologist

kindly—but Mrs. Fontenette was by this time tired, and she never again felt rested when her husband mentioned the game.

Furthermore, their countenances!—hers and the entomologist's—especially when in repose—you could read the depths of experience they had sounded, by the lines and shadows that came and went, or stayed, as one may read the depths of a bay by the passing of wind and light, day by day, over its waters—particularly if the waters are not very deep.

They made painful reading. What degrees of heart-wretchedness came and went or stayed with them, we may have over— we may have underestimated. God knows. In two months Mrs. Fontenette grew visibly older and less pretty, yet more nearly beautiful; while he, by every sign, was gradually awakening back—or, shall we not say, being now first born?—to life, through the pangs of a torn mind; mind, not conscience; but pangs never of sated, always of the famished sort.

XII

IT was he who finally put the very seal
of confirmation upon both our hopes and
our fears.

The time was the evening of the same
Sunday in whose afternoon his wife had
declined those transparent spelling-lessons.
A certain preacher, noted for his boldness,
was drawing crowds by a series of sermons
on the text " Be thou clean," and our fat
neighbor and his wife took us, all six, to
hear him. Their pew was well to the front
and we were late, so that going down the
aisle unushered, with them in the lead—
husband and spouse, husband and spouse,
four couples—we made a procession which
became embarrassingly amusing as the
preacher simultaneously closed the Scrip-
ture lesson with, " And Noah went in, and
his sons, and his wife, and his sons' wives
with him into the ark."

That has been our fat neighbor's best joke
ever since, though he always says after it,
" The poor Baron! " and often adds—" and

The Entomologist

poor Mrs. Fontenette! Little did we think,"
etc. But he has never even suspected their
secret.

The entomologist was the last of our pew-
full to give heed to the pulpit. When the
preacher said that because it was a year of
state elections, for which we ought already
to be preparing, he had in his first discourse
touched upon political purity—cleanness of
citizenship—the Baron showed no interest.
He still showed none when the speaker said
again, that because the pestilence was once
more with us—that was in the terrible visi-
tation of 1878—he had devoted his second
discourse to the hideous crime of a great
city whose voters and tax-payers do not
enable and compel it to keep the precept,
" Be thou clean." I thought of the clean
little home from whose master beside me
came no evidence that he thought at all.
But the moment the preacher declared his
purpose to consider now the application of
this great command to the individual life
and character of man and woman as simply
man and woman, the entomologist became
the closest listener in the crowded throng.

The sermon was a daring one. I was struck by the shrewd concessions with which the speaker defined personal purity and the various false conceptions of it that pass current; abandoning the entrenched hills, so to speak, of his church's traditional rigor and of many conventional rules, and drawing after him into the unfortified plain his least persuadable hearers of whatever churchly or unchurchly prejudice, to surround them finally at one wide sweep and receive their unconditional surrender. His periods were not as embarrassing to a mixed audience as my citations would indicate. Those that I bring together were wisely subordinated and kept apart in the discourse, and ran together only in minds like my own, eager for one or two other hearers to be specially impressed by them. And one, at least, was. Before the third sentence of the main discourse was finished the fierceness of the Baron's attention was provoking me to ask myself whether a conscience also was not coming to birth in him.

In a spiritual-material being, said the speaker, the spirit has a rightful, happy

The Entomologist

share in every physical delight, and no physical delight need be unclean in which the spirit can freely enjoy its just share as senior member in the partnership of soul and body. Without this spiritual participation it could not be clean, though church, state, and society should jointly approve and command it. Mark, I do not answer for the truth of these things; I believe them, but that is quite outside of our story.

The commonest error, he said, of those who covet spiritual cleanness is to seek a purification of self for self-purification's sake.

The Baron grunted. He was drinking in the words; had forgotten his surroundings.

Only those are clean, continued the speaker, whose every act, motive, condition is ordered according to their best knowledge of the general happiness, whether that happiness is for the time embodied in millions, or in but one beyond themselves. Through errors of judgment they may fall into manifest outward uncleannesses; but they, and none but they, are clean within.

Because women, he went on, are in every way more delicately made than men, we easily take it for granted they are more spiritual. From Genesis to Revelation the Bible never does so. It is amazing how feeble a sense of condemnation women— even as compared with men—often show for the *spirit* of certain misdeeds if only it be unaccompanied by the misdeed's performance; or what loathing so many of them—"of you," he really said, and the Baron grunted as though his experience had been with droves of them—what loathing so many of you heap upon certain things without reference to the spirit by which they are accompanied and on which their nobility or baseness, their cleanness or foulness, entirely depends.

Nothing is unclean that is to no one anywhere unjust or unkind; and nothing is unjust, unkind, or unclean which cannot easily be shown to be so without inventing an eleventh commandment. To him, he said, no uncleanness was more foul than that which, not for kindness, or for righteousness, but for a fantastical, self-centred re-

finement, invents some eleventh commandment to call that common which God hath
cleansed; to call anything brutish which the
incarnation of the soul has made sacred to
spotless affections.

The Baron muttered something in German, and Fontenette shut his mouth tight
and straightened up in approbation.

At the close of the service we were not
out of the pew before our escort was introducing Senda to his friends in front and
behind as busily and elaborately as if that
was what we had come for. Twice and
again she cast so anxious an eye upon her
husband—from whom Mrs. Fontenette had
wisely taken shelter behind hers—that I
softly said to her, " We'll take care of him."

A care he was! All the way down the
aisle, amid the peals of the organ, he com-
mented on the sermon aloud, mostly to himself but also to whichever of us he could
rub his glasses against. Sometimes he
mistook others for us until they stared. His
face showed a piteous, weary distress, his
thin hair went twenty ways, he seemed
scarcely to know where he was or how to

take his steps, and presently was saying to a strange lady crowded against him, as though it was with her he had been talking all along:

"Undt vhy shall ve haf t'at owfool troubple? No-o, t'at vould kill me! I am not a cat to keep me alvays clean—no more as a hogk to keep me always not clean. No, I keep me—owdside—inside—always so clean as it comes eassy, undt I leave me so dirty as it comes eassy."

XIII

I TOOK his arm into mine—his hand was hot—and drew him on alone. "Undt t'ose vomens," he persisted in the vestibule, " t'ey are more troubple yet as t'eir veight in goldt! I vish, mine Gott! t'ere be no more any vomens ut all, undt ve haf t'e shiltern by mutchinery."

On the outer steps I sprang with others to save a young girl, who had stumbled, from pitching headlong to the sidewalk. Once on her feet again, after a limp or two she walked away uninjured; but when I looked around for my real charge he was not in sight. I hurried to Fontenette and his wife a few steps away, but he was not with them. The three of us turned back and came upon the rest of our group, but neither had they seen him. Our other neighbor said he must have got into a car. I asked Senda if it was likely he would go home without trying to find us, and she replied that he might; but when we had all looked at one another for a moment she added, with a distinct tremor of voice—and I saw that she feared temptation and conscience had unsettled his wits—" I sink he iss not ve'y vell. I sink he is maybe—I ton't know, but—I—I sink he iss not ve'y vell." She averted her face.

She agreed with us, of course, that there was no call for alarm, and Mrs. Smith and I had to plead that we could not, the six of us, let her go home, away downtown, alone, while we should go as far the other way and remain all night ignorant of her husband's whereabouts. So our next door neighbor, my wife and I went with her, and

his wife and the Fontenettes went home;
for a conviction probably common to us all,
but which no one cared to put into down-
right words, was that the entomologist,
whether dazed or not, might wander up to
one of our homes in preference to his own.
In the street-car and afterward for a full
hour at her house, Senda was very silent,
only saying now a little and then a little
more.

"*He* iss all right! *He* vill sure come.
Many times he been avay se *whole* night.
Sat is se first time I am eveh afraid; is sat
se vay when commencing to grow old?
Yes, I sink sat is se reason."

When we had been at her cottage for
nearly an hour, my neighbor started out
on a systematic search; and half an hour
later, I left Mrs. Smith with her and went
also.

About one o'clock in the night, I came
back as far as the corner nearest her house,
but waited there, by appointment, with my
neighbor; and very soon—stepping softly
—he appeared.

"No sign of him?"

The Entomologist

"None."

"You don't suppose he's done himself any violence, do you?" he asked.

"No, no. O no."

"And yet," he said, "I think we ought to tell the police at once."

I advanced some obvious objections. "At any rate," I said, "go in, will you, please, and see if he hasn't come home, while we were away."

"Why, yes, that *is* the first thing," laughed he, and went.

As I waited for him in the still street, I heard far away a quick footstep. By and by I saw a man pass under a distant lamp, coming toward me. I looked with all my eyes. Just then my neighbor came back. "Listen," I murmured. "Watch when that man comes under the next light."

He watched. "It's Fontenette!"

"Well," said the Creole as he joined us, "he's yondeh all right—except sick.

"Yes, he cou'n't tell anybody where to take him, and a doctor found that letteh on him print' outside with yo' uptown address; and so he put him in a cab an' sen' him

yondeh, and sen' word he muz 'ave been
sick sinze sev'l hours, an' get him in bed
quick don't lose a minute."

" And so he's in bed at my house!" I put
in approvingly.

"Ah, no! I coul'n' do like that; but I
do the bes' I could; he is at *my* 'ouse in bed.
An' my own doctor sen' word what to do
an' he'll come in the mawning. And (to
our neighbor) yo' madame do uz that kine-
ness to remain with Madame Fontenette
whiles I'm bringing his wife."

At the cottage my companions remained
outside. As I entered Senda caught one
glance and exclaimed, " Ah, mine hussbandt is foundt andt is anyhow alife!"

" Yes," I replied, " but he's ill. Mr. Fontenette met him and took him to his house.
He's there now with Mrs. Fontenette and
Mrs. Blank. Get a change of dress and
come, we'll all go together."

Senda stared. " A shange of dtress?"
Then, with a most significant mingling of
relief and new disturbance, she said, " Ah,
I see!" and looking from me to Mrs. Smith
and from Mrs. Smith to me, while she

whipped her bonnet ribbons into a bow, she cried, with shaking voice and streaming eyes:

"Oh, sank Kott! sank Kott! it iss only se yellow feveh."

XIV

No sick man could have been better cared for than was the entomologist at our neighbor's over the way. "The fever," as in the Creole city it used to be sufficiently distinguished, is not so deadly, nor so treacherous, nor nearly so repulsive, as some other maladies, but none requires closer attention. After successive days and nights of unremitting vigilance, should there occur a momentary closing of the nurse's eyes, or a turning from the bedside for a quarter of a minute, the irresponsible patient may attempt to rise and may fall back dying or dead. So, the attendant must have an attendant. In the case of the entomologist, his wife became the bedside nurse and sentinel.

Strong Hearts

In the next room, now and then Mrs.
Smith, and now and then our fat neighbor's
wife, waited on her, but by far the most of
the time, Mrs. Fontenette was her assistant.
When Senda, while the patient dozed, stole
brief moments of sleep to keep what she
could of her overtasked powers, her place,
at the bedside, was always filled by Fontenette, who as often kept his promise to
call her the instant her husband should
rouse.

Thus we brought our precious entomologist through the disorder's first crisis,
which generally comes exactly on the sev-
enty-second hour, and in due time through
the second, which falls, if I remember aright,
on the ninth day. What I do recall with
certainty, was that it came on one of the
days of the city's heaviest mortality and that
two of our children, and my next neighbor's
wife, came down with the scourge.

And O, the beautiful days and the beautiful nights! It seemed the illusion of a
dream, that between such land and sky,
there should be not one street in that em-
bowered city unsmitten by sorrow and

death. Out of yonder fair home on the right, they carried yesterday, the loved mother of five children—but the Baron is better. From this one on the left, will be borne to-morrow such a man as no city can lightly spare, till now a living fulfilment of the word " Be thou clean "—but the entomologist will be ever so much better.

To be glad of it, you needed only to hear Senda allude to him as " Mine hussbandt." Why did she never mention him in any other way? The little woman was a riddle to me. I did not see how she could give such a man such a love, and yet I never could see but she was as frank as a public record. Stranger still was it how she could be the marital partner—the mate, to speak plainly—of such a one, without showing or feeling the slightest spiritual debasement. Finally, however, I caught some light. I had stepped over to ask after " Mine hussbandt," everyone else of us being busy with our own sick. Senda was letting Fontenette take her place in the sick-room, which, of course, was shut close. I silently entered the room in front of it, and perceiving that

Mrs. Fontenette had drawn her into the other front room, adjoining—a door stood half open between—and was tempting her with refreshments, I sat down to await their next move. So presently I began to hear what they said to each other in their gentle speculations.

" A wife who has realized her ideal," Mrs. Fontenette was saying, when Senda interrupted:

" Ah! vhat vife is sat? In vhat part of se vorldt does she lif, and how long she is marriedt? No-o, no! Sare is only vun *kindt* of vife in se *whole* vorldt vhat realize her ideal hussbandt; and sat is se vife vhat idealize her real hussbandt. Also not se hussbandt and se vife only; I sink you even cannot much Christ-yanity practice vis anybody—close related—vissout you idealize sem. But ze hussbandt and vife—

" You remembeh sat sehmon, ' Be '—O yes, of course. Vell, sat is vun sing se preacher forget to say—May be he haf not se time, but I sink he forget: sat sare is no hussbandt in se whole vorldt—and also sare is no vife—so sp'—spirit'—spirited? no?

156

The Entomologist

Ah, yes—spiritual!—yes, sank you. Vhen I catch me a bigk vord I am so proudt, yet, as I hadt a fish caught!"

I was willing to believe it, but thought how still more true it was of Mrs. Fontenette. But the gentle speaker had not paused. "Sare iss no vife so *spiritual*," she repeated, triumphantly, "and who got a hussbandt so spiritual, sat eeser vun—do you say 'eeser vun'?"

"Either one," said her hostess, reassuringly.

"Yes, so spiritual sat eeser vun can keep sat rule inside—to be pairfect' clean, if sat vun do not see usseh vun *idealize*."

I made a stir—"Hmm!" Whereupon she came warily to the door. I sat engrossed in a book and wishing I could silently crawl under it snake fashion; but I could feel her eyes all over me, and with them was a glimmering smile that helped them to make me tingle as she softly spoke.

"Ah! See se book-vorm! He iss all eyes—and ee-ahs. Iss it *not* so?"

"Pardon," I murmured; "did you spe'

—has any one been speaking and I have failed to give attention?"

"O no, sir! I sink not! Vell, you are velcome to all you haf heardt; but I am ve'y much oblige' to you for yo' 'hmm.' It vas se right sing in se right place. But do you not sink I shouldt haf been a pre-eacheh? I love to preach."

I said I knew of three men in one neighborhood with whom she might start a church, and asked how was the Baron.

Improving—would soon be able to sit up. She inquired after my children.

It was quite in accord with a late phase of Mrs. Fontenette's demeanor that on this occasion she did not appear until I mentioned her. She had not come near me by choice since the night the Baron was found and sent to my address, although I certainly was in every way as nice to her as I had ever been, and I was not expecting now to be less so.

When she appeared I asked her if a superb rose blooming late in August was not worth crossing to our side of the way to see. She knew, of course, that sooner or later, as the best of a bad choice, she must allow me an interview; yet now she was about to decline on some small excuse, when her eyes met mine, and she saw that in my opinion the time had come. So she made her excuses to her guest and went with me.

She gave the rose generous notice and praise, and as she led the way back lingered admiringly over flower after flower. Yet she said little; more than once she paused entirely to let me if I chose change the subject, and when at the gate I did so, she stood like a captive, looking steadily into my face with eyes as helpless as a halffledged bird's and as lovely as its mother's. When I drew something from my breastpocket, they did not move.

"This," I said, "is the letter that was found on the Baron the night he was taken ill. Your husband handed it to me supposing, of course, I had written it, as it was in one of my envelopes, and he happens not to know my handwriting. But I did not write it. I had never seen it, yet it was sent in one of my envelopes. I haven't mentioned it to anyone else, because—you see?—I hope you do. I thought—well, frankly, I thought if I should mention it first to you I might never need to mention it to anyone else." I waited a moment and then asked, eyes and all: " Who could have sent it?"

" Isn't," she began, but her voice failed, and when it came again it was hardly more than a whisper, " isn't it signed?"

Now, that was just what I did not know. Whatever the thing was, I had never taken it from the envelope. But the moment she asked I knew. I knew it bore no signature. We gazed into each other's eyes for many seconds until hers tried to withdraw. Then I said—and the words seemed to drop from my lips unthought—" It didn't have to be signed, Mrs. Fontenette, although the hand-writing is disguised."

Poor Flora! I can but think, even yet, I was kinder than if I had been kind; but it was brutal, and I felt myself a brute, thus to be holding her up to herself there on the open sidewalk where she dared not even weep or wring her hands or hide her face, but only make idle marks on the brick pavement with her tiny boots—and tremble.

" I—I had to write it," she began to reply, and her words, though they quivered, were as mechanical as mine. " He was so—so—imprudent—my husband's happiness required——"

I stopped her. " Please don't say that, Mrs. Fontenette. Pardon me, but—not that, please." I felt for an instant quite cruel enough to have told her what ebb tides she had given that husband's happiness; what he had been so near doing and had been led back from only by the absolute christliness of that other woman and wife, whose happiness scarcely seemed ever to have occurred to her; but that was his secret, not mine.

She broke a silence with a suppressed exclamation of pain, while for the eyes of possible observers I imitated her in a nonchalant pose. " You wouldn't despise me if you knew the half I've suffered or how I've striv—— "

I interrupted again. " O Mrs. Fontenette, any true gentleman—at thirty-five—

knows it *all—himself*. And he had better go and cut his throat than give himself airs, even of pity, over a lady who has made a misstep she cannot retrace."

Her foot played with a brick that was loose in the pavement, but she gave me a melting glance of gratitude. After a considerable pause she murmured, " I will retrace it."

" I have kept you here a good while," I said. " After a moment or so drop your handkerchief, and as I return it to you the letter will be with it. Or, better, if you choose to trust me, we'll not do that, but as soon as I get into the house I'll burn it."

" I can trust you," she replied, " but——"

" What; the Baron—when he misses it? O I'll settle that."

She gave a start as though I had shouted. I thought it a bad sign for the future, and the words that followed seemed to me worse. " Isn't it my duty," she asked—and her eyes betrayed unconsciously the desperateness of her desire—" to explain to him myself?"

I answered with a question. " Would

that be in the line of retracement, Mrs. Fontenette?"

"It would!" she responded, with solemn eagerness. "O it would be! It shall be! I promise you!"

"Mrs. Fontenette," said I, "consider. If his wife"—she flinched; she could do so now, for the sudden semi-tropical darkness had fallen—"if his wife—or your husband"—she bit her lip—"knew all—would they think that your duty? Would it take them an instant to refuse their consent? Would they not firmly insist that it is your duty never again to see him alone?"

Her only reply was an involuntary moan and a whitening of the face, and for the first time I saw how deep into her soul the poison had gone.

"My friend," I continued, "you must not think me meddlesome—officious. I can no more wait for your permission to help you than if you were drowning. Perhaps for good reasons within *me*, I know, better than you, that you—and he—are on a slippery incline, and that whether you can stop your descent and creep back to higher ground than either of you has slipped from is not to be told by the fineness of your promises or resolves. I cannot tell; you cannot tell; only God knows." . . .

"Please, sir," said a new maid—in place of one who had gone home fever-struck and had died—"yo' lady saunt me fo' to tell you yo' little boy a sett'n on de back steps an' sayin' his head does ache him, an' she wish you'd 'ten' to him, 'caze she cayn't leave his lill' sisteh, 'caze she threaten with convulsion'."

XV

Mrs. Fontenette and the maid silently ran in ahead of me; I went first to the mother. When I found Mrs. Fontenette again she had the child undressed and in his crib, and I remembered how often I had, in my heart, called her a coward.

She saw me pencil on a slip of paper at the mantelpiece, and went and read—" You mustn't stay. He has the fever. You've never had it."

164

The Entomologist

She wrote beneath—" I should have got it weeks ago if God paid wages every day. Don't turn me off."

I dropped the paper into the small fire-grate, added the other from my breast-pocket, and set them ablaze, and the new maid, entering, praised burning paper as one of the best deodorizers known.

So my dainty rose-neighbor stayed; stayed all night, and all the next day and night, and on and on with only flying visits to her home over the way, until we were amazed at her endurance. The little fellow was never at ease with her out of his wild eyes. Her touch was balm to him, and her words peace. Oh, that they might have been healing also! But that was beyond the reach of all our striving. His days were as the flowers and winged things of the garden-kingdom, wherein he had been—without ever guessing it—their citizen-king.

It awakens all the tenderness at once that I ever had for Mrs. Fontenette, to recall what she was to him in those hours, and to us when his agonies were all past, and he lay so stately on his short bier, and she could not be done going to it and looking —looking—with streaming eyes.

As she stood close by the tomb, while we dumbly watched the masons seal it, I began to believe that she blamed herself for the child's sickness and death, and presently I knew it must be so. One of those quaint burial societies of Negro women, in another quarter of the grounds, but within plain hearing, chose for the ending of their burial service—with what fitness to their burial service I cannot say, maybe none—a hymn borrowed, I judge, from the rustic whites, as usual, but Africanized enough to thrill the dullest nerves ; and the moment it began my belief was confirmed.

My sin is so dahk, Lawd, so dahk and so deep,
  My grief is so po', Lawd, so po' and so mean,
I wisht I could weep, Lawd, I wisht I could weep,
  Oh, I wisht I could weep like Mary Mahgaleen!

Oh, Sorroh! sweet Sorroh! come, welcome, and
    stay!
  I'd welcome thy swode howsomever so keen,
If I could jes' pray, Lawd, if I could jes' pray,
  Oh! if I could jes' pray, like Mary Mahgaleen!

The Entomologist

My belief was confirmed, I say; but I was glad to see also that no one else read as I read the signs by which I was guided. At the cemetery gate I heard some one call— "Yo' madam is sick, sih," and, turning, saw Mrs. Fontenette, deathly white, lift her blue eyes to her husband and he get his arm about her just in time to save her from falling. She swooned but a moment, and, in the carriage, before it started off, tried to be quite herself, though very pale.

"It's nothing but the reaction," said to me the lady who fanned her, and we agreed it was a wonder she had held up so long.

"Hyeh, honey," put in the child's old black nurse, in a voice that never failed to soothe, however grotesque its misinterpretations, "lay yo' head on me; an' lay it heavy: dass what I'm use-en to. Blessed is de pyo in haht; she shall res' in de fea' o' de Lawd, an' he shall lafe at heh calamity."

I was glad to send the old woman with them, for as we turned away to our own carriage, I said in my mind, "All that little lady needs is enough contrition, and she'll give away the total of any secret of which she owns an undivided half."

But a night and a day passed, and a second, and a third, and I perceived she had told nothing.

It was a terrible time, with many occasions of suspense more harrowing than that. Our other children were getting on, yet still needed vigilant care; the Baron was to be let out of his room in a day or two, but my fat neighbor had come down with the disease, while his wife still lay between life and death—how they finally got well, I have never quite made out, they were so badly nursed—and all about us were new cases, and cases beyond hope, and retarded recoveries, and relapses, and funerals, and nurses too few, and ice scarce, and everybody worn out with watching—physicians compelled to limit themselves to just so many cases at a time, to avoid utterly breaking down.

As I was in my fat neighbor's sick chamber one evening, giving his nurse a respite, word came that Fontenette was at my gate. I went to him with misgivings that only increased as we greeted. He was dejected and agitated. His grasp was damp and cold.

"It cou'n' stay from me always," he said in an anguished voice, and I cried in my soul, "She's told him!"

But she had not. I asked him what his bad news was that had come at last, but his only reply was,

"Can you take *him?* Can you take him out of my house—to-night—this evening—now?"

"Who, the Baron? Why, certainly, if you desire it?" I responded; wondering if the entomologist, by some slip, had betrayed *her*. There was an awe in my visitor's eyes that was almost fright.

"Fontenelle," I exclaimed, "what have you heard—what have you done?"

"My frien', 'tis not what I 'ave heard, neitheh what I 'ave done; 'tis what I 'ave got."

"Got? Why, you've got nothing, you Creole of the Creoles. Your skin's as cool as mine."

"Feel my pulse," he said. I felt it. It wasn't less than a hundred and fifty.

"Go, get into bed while I bring the Baron over here," I said, and by the time I had done this and got back to him his skin was hot enough! An hour or two after, I recrossed the street on the way to my night's rest, leaving his wife to nurse him, and Senda to attend on her and keep house. I paused in the garden and gazed up among the benignant stars. And then I looked onward, through and beyond their ranks, seemingly so confused, yet where such amazing hidden order is, and said, for our good Fontenette, and for his watching wife, and for all of us—even for my wife and me in our unutterable loss—" Sank Kott! sank Kott! it iss only se yellow fevah!"

XVI

THREE days more. In the third evening I found the doctor saying to Mrs. Fontenette: "Nine o'clock. It's now seven-thirty. Well, you'd better begin pretty soon to watch for the change.

"O, you'll know it when you see it, it will

The Entomologist

be as plain as something sinking in water right before your eyes. Then give him the beef-tea, just a teaspoonful; then, by and by, another, and another, as I told you, always keeping his head on the pillow—mind that."

Out beside his carriage he continued to me: " O yes, a nurse or patient may break that rule, or almost any rule, and the patient may live. I had a patient, left alone for a moment on the climacteric day, who was found standing at her mirror combing her hair, and to-day she's as well as you or I. I had another who got out of bed, walked down a corridor, fell face downward and lay insensible at the crack of a doorsill with the rain blowing in on him under the door —and he got well. As to Fontenette, all his symptoms so far are good. Well—I'll be back in the morning."

So ran the time. There were no more new cases in our house; Mrs. Smith and I had had the scourge years before, as also had Senda, who remained over the way. Fontenette passed from one typical phase of the disorder to another " charmingly " as the doctor said, yet he specially needed just such exceptionally delicate care as his wife was giving him. In the city at large the deaths per day were more and more, and one night when it showered and there was a heavenly cooling of the air, the increase in the mortality was horrible. But the weather, as a rule, was steady and tropically splendid; the sun blazed; the moonlight was marvellous; the dews were like rains; the gardens were gay with butterflies. Our convalescent little ones hourly forgot how gravely far they were from being well, and it became one of our heavy cares to keep the entomologist from entomologizing—and from overeating.

From time to time, when shorthanded we had used skilled nurses; but when Mrs. Fontenette grew haggard and we mentioned them, she said distressfully: " O! no hireling hands! I can't bear the thought of it! " and indeed the thought of the average hired " fever-nurse " of those days was not inspiring; so I served as her alternate when she would accept any and throw herself on the couch Senda had spread in the little parlor.

The Entomologist

XVII

AT length one day I was called up at dawn and went over to take her place once more, and when after several hours had passed I was still with him, Fontenette said, while I bent down,

"I have the fear thad's going to go hahd with my wife, being of the Nawth."

"Why, what's going to go hard, old fellow?"

"The feveh. My dear frien', don't I know tha'z the only thing would keep heh f'om me thad long?"

"Still, you don't know her case will be a hard one; it may be very light. But don't talk now."

"Well—I hope *so*. Me, I wou'n' take ten thousand dollahs faw thad feveh myself—to see that devotion of my wife. You muz 'ave observe', eh?"

"Yes, indeed, old man; nobody could help observing. I wouldn't talk any more just now."

"No," he insisted, "nobody could eveh

doubt. 'Action speak loudeh than word,' eh?"

"Yes, but we don't want either from you just now." I put his restless arms back under the cover; not to keep the outer temperature absolutely even was counted a deadly risk. "Besides," I said, "you're talking out of character, old boy."

He looked at me mildly, steadily, for several moments, as if something about me gave him infinite comfort. It was a man's declaration of love to a man, and as he read the same in my eyes, he closed his own and drowsed.

Though he dozed only at wide intervals and briefly, he asked no more questions until night; then—"Who's with my wife?"

"Mine."

He closed his eyes again, peacefully. It was in keeping with his perfect courtesy not to ask how the new patient was. If she was doing well,—well; and if not, he would spare us the pain of informing or deceiving him.

Senda became a kind of chief-of-staff for both sides of the street. She would have

begged to be Mrs. Fontenette's nurse, but
for one other responsibility, which we felt
it would be unsafe, and she thought it would
be unfair, for her to put thus beyond her
own reach: " se care of mine hussbandt."

She wore a plain path across the unpaved
street to our house, and another to our
neighbor's. " Sat iss a too great risk," she
compassionately maintained, " to leaf even
in se daytime sose shiltren—so late sick—
alone viss only mine hussbandt and se sairvants! "

The doctor was concerned for Mrs. Fontenette from the beginning. " Terribly nervous," he said, " and full from her feet to
her eyes, of a terror of death—merely a part
of the disease, you know." But in this case
I did not know.

" Pathetic," he called the fevered satis-
faction she took in the hovering attentions
of our old black nurse, who gave us brief
respites in the two sick-rooms by turns, and
who had according to Mrs. Fontenette,
" such a beautiful faith! " The doctor
thought it mostly words, among which
" de Lawd willin' " so constantly recurred

that out of the sick-room he always alluded
to her as D. V., though never without a
certain sincere regard. This kind old soul
had nursed much yellow fever in her time,
and it did not occur to us that maybe her
time was past.

When Mrs. Fontenette had been ill something over a week, the doctor one evening
made us glad by saying as he came through
the little dining-room and jerked a thumb
back toward Fontenette's door, " Just keep
him as he is for one more night and, I
promise you, he'll get well; but! "— He
sat down on the couch—Senda's—in the
parlor, and pointed at the door to Mrs. Fontenette's room—" You've got to be careful
how you let even that be known—in there!
She can get well too—if—" And he went
on to tell how in this ailment all the tissues
of the body sink into such frail deteriora-
tion, that so slight a thing as the undue
thrill of an emotion, may rend some inner
part of the soul's house and make it hopelessly untenable.

" Iss sat not se condition vhat make it
so easy to relapse?" asked Senda.

The Entomologist

He said it was, I think, and went his way,
little knowing to what a night he was leaving us—except for its celestial beauty, upon
which he expatiated as I stepped with him
to the gate.

XVIII

He had not been gone long enough for
me to get back into the house—Fontenette's—when I espied coming to me, in
piteous haste from her home around the
corner, the young daughter of another
neighbor. Her hair was about her eyes and
as she saw the physician had gone, she
wrung her hands and burst into violent
weeping. I ran to her outside the gate,
pointing backward at Mrs. Fontenette's
room, with entreating signs for quiet as she
called—" Oh, *where* is he gone? Which
way did he go?"

"I can't tell you, my dear girl!" I murmured. "I don't know! What is the
trouble?"

"My father!" she hoarsely whispered.

" My father's dying! dying in a raging delirium, and we can't hold him in bed! O, come and help us!" She threw her hands above her head in wild despair, and gnawed her fingers and lips and shook and writhed as she gulped down her sobs, and laid hold of me and begged as though I had refused.

I found her words true. It took four men to keep him down. I did not have to stay to the end, and when I reached Fontenette's side again, was glad to find I had been away but little over an hour.

I sent the old black woman home and to bed, and may have sat an hour more, when she came back to tell us, that one of the children was very wakeful and feverish. Senda went to see into the matter for us, and the old woman took her place in the little parlor. Mrs. Smith was with Mrs. Fontenette.

Fontenette slept. Loath to see him open his eyes, I kept very still, while nearly another hour dragged by, listening hard for Senda's return, but hearing only, once or twice, through the narrow stairway and closets between the two bedrooms, a faint stir that showed Mrs. Fontenette was awake and being waited on.

I was grateful for the rarity of outdoor sounds; a few tree-frogs piped, two or three solitary wayfarers passed in the street; twice or more the sergeant of the night-watch trilled his whistle in a street or two behind us, and twice or more in front; and once, and once again, came the distant bellow of steamboats passing each other—not the famous boats whose whistle you would know one from another, for they were laid up. I doubt if I have forgotten any sound that I noticed that night. I remember the drowsy rumble of the midnight horse-car and tinkle of its mule's bell, first in Prytania street and then in Magazine. It was just after these that at last a black hand beckoned me to the door, and under her breath the old nurse told me she was just back from our house, where her mistress had sent her, and that—" De-eh—de-eh "—

" The Baroness? "

" Yass, sih, de—de outlayndish la-ady—"

Senda had sent word that the child had

only an indigestion—a thing serious enough in such a case—and though still slightly feverish was now asleep, but restless.

"Sih? Yass, sir—awnressless—dass 'zac'-ly what I say!"

Wherefore Senda would either remain in the nursery or return to us, as we should elect.

"O no, sih, she no need to come back right now, anyhow; yass, sih, dass what de Mis' say, too."

"Then you'll stay here," I whispered.

"Yass, sih, ef de Lawd wil'—I mean ef you wants me, sih—yass, sih, thaynk you, sih. I loves to tend on Mis' Fontenette, she got sich a bu'ful fa-aith, same like she say I got. Yass, sih, I dess loves to set an' watch her—wid dat sweet samtimonious fa-ace."

Fontenette being still asleep I gave her my place for a moment, and went to the door between the parlor and his wife's room. Mrs. Smith came to it, barely breathing the triumphant word—"Just dropped asleep!"

When I replied that I would take a little

fresh air at the front door she asked if at
my leisure I would empty and bring in from
the window-sill, around on the garden side
of her patient's room a saucer containing
the over-sweetened remains of some orange-
leaf tea, that " D. V." had made " for to
wrench out de nerves." She wanted the
saucer.

I went outside a step or two and took in
a long draught of good air—the air of a
yellow-fever room is dreadful. It was my
first breath of mental relief also; almost the
first that night, and the last.

I paced once or twice the short narrow
walk between the front flower-beds, surprised at their well-kept and blooming condition until I remembered Senda. The
moths were out in strong numbers, and it
was delightful to forget graver things for a
moment and see the flowers bend coyly under their passionate kisses and blushingly
rise again when the sweet robbery was finished. So it happened that I came where a
glance across to my own garden showed
me, on the side farthest from the nursery,
a favorite bush, made pale by a light that

could come only from the entomologist's
window! I went in promptly, told what I
proposed to do, and hurried out again.

XIX

I crossed into my garden and silently
mounted the balcony stairs I have mentioned once before. His balcony door was
ajar. His room was empty. He had occupied the bed. A happy thought struck me
—to feel the spot where he had lain; it was
still warm. Good! But his clothes were
all gone except his shoes, and they, you remember, were no proof that he was indoors.

I stole down into the garden once more,
and looked hurriedly in several directions,
but saw no sign of him. I am not a ferocious man even when alone, but as I came
near the fence of our fat neighbor—once
fat, poor fellow, and destined to be so again
in time—and still saw no one, I was made
conscious of waving my fist and muttering
through my gritting teeth, by hearing my
name softly called. It was an unfamiliar

The Entomologist

female voice that spoke, from a window beyond the fence, and it flashed on my remembrance that two kinswomen of my neighbor were watching with his wife, whose case was giving new cause for anxiety. It was Mrs. Soandso, the voice explained, and could I possibly come in there a moment?—if only to the window!

"Is our friend the Baron over here?" I asked, as I came to it. He was not. "Well, never mind," I said; "how is your patient?"

"Oh that's just what we wish we knew. In some ways she seems better, but she's more unquiet. She's had some slight nausea and it seems to increase. Do you think that is important?"

"Yes," I said, "very. I hear some one cracking ice; you are keeping ice on her throat—no? Well, begin it at once, and persuade her to lie on her back as quietly as she can, and get her to sleep if possible! Doctor—no; he wouldn't come before morning, anyhow; but I'll send Mrs. Smith right over to you, if she possibly can come."

I turned hurriedly away and had taken only a few steps, when I lit upon the entomologist. "Well, I'll just—what *are* you doing here? Where were you when I was in your room just now?" His shoes were on.

"Vhat you vanted mit me? I vas by dot librair' going. For vhat you moof dot putterfly-net fon t'e mandtelpiece? You make me *too* much troubple to find dot vhen I vas in a hurry!" He shook it at me.

"Hurry!" In my anger and distress I laughed. "My friend"—laying a hand on him—"you'll hurry across the street with me."

He waved me off. "Yes; go on, you; I coom py undt py; I dtink t'ere iss vun maud come into dot gardten, vhat I haf not pefore seen since more as acht years, alreadty!"

"Yes," I retorted, "and so you're here at the gate alone. Now come right along with me! Aren't there enough lives in danger to-night, but you must"—He stopped me in the middle of the street.

"Mine Gott! vhat iss dot you say? Who —*who*—mine Gott! *who* iss her life in dtanger? Iss dot—mine Gott! is dot he-ere?"

The Entomologist

He pointed to Mrs. Fontenette's front window.

I could hardly keep my fist off him. "Hush! you— For one place it's *here*." I pushed him with my finger.

"Ach!" he exclaimed in infinite relief. "I dt'ought you mean—I—I dt'ought— hmm!—hmm! Iam dtired." He leaned on me like a sick child and we went into the cottage parlor. The moment he saw the lounge he lay down upon it, or I should have taken him back into the dining-room.

"Sha'n't I put that net away for you?" I murmured, as I dropped a light covering over him.

But he only hugged the toy closer. "No; I geep it—hmm!—hmm!—I am dtired——"

XX

BOTH patients, I found, were drowsing; the husband peacefully, the wife with troubled dreams. When the Baron spoke her eyes opened with a look, first eager and then distressful, but closed again. We put the old black woman temporarily into her room and Mrs. Smith hurried to our other neighbors, whence she was to despatch one of their servants to bid Senda come to us at once. But " No battle "—have I already used the proverb? She gave the message to the servant, but it never reached Senda. Somebody forgot. As I sat by Fontenette with ears alert for Senda's coming and was wondering at the unbroken silence, he opened his eyes on me and smiled.

" Ah! " he softly said, " thad was a pleasan' dream! "

" A pleasant dream, was it? "

" Yes; I was having the dream thad my wife she was showing me those rose-*bushes;* an' every rose-*bush* it had roses, an' every rose it was perfect."

The Entomologist

I leaned close and said that he had been
mighty good not to ask about her all these
many days, and that if he would engage to
do as well for as long a time again, and to
try now to have another good dream I
would tell him that she was sleeping and
was without any alarming symptoms. O
lucky speech! It was true when it was
uttered; but how soon the hour belied it!

As he obediently closed his eyes, his hand
stole out from the side of the covers and
felt for mine. I gave it and as he kept it
his thought seemed to me to flow into my
brain. I could feel him, as it were, thinking of his wife, loving her through all the
deeps of his still nature with seven—yes,
seventy—times the passion that I fancied
would ever be possible to that young girl
I had seen a few hours earlier showing her
heart to the world, with falling hair and
rending sobs. As he lay thus trying to
court back his dream of perfect roses, I had
my delight in knowing he would never
dream—what Senda saw so plainly, yet with
such faultless modesty—that all true love
draws its strength and fragrance from the

187

riches not of the loved one's, but of the lover's soul.

His grasp had begun to loosen, when I thought I heard from the wife's room a sudden sound that made my mind flash back to the saucer I had failed to bring in. It was as though the old-fashioned, unweighted window-sash, having been slightly lifted, had slipped from the fingers and fallen shut. I hearkened, and the next instant there came softly searching through doors, through walls, through my own flesh and blood, a long half-wailing sigh. Fontenette tightened on my hand, then dropped it, and opening his eyes sharply, asked, "What was that?"

"What was what, old fellow?" I pretended to have been more than half asleep myself.

"Did I only dream I 'eard it, thad noise?"

"That isn't a hard thing to do in your condition," I replied, with my serenest smile, and again he closed his eyes. Yet for two or three minutes it was plain he listened; but soon he forbore and began once

more to slumber. Then very soon I faintly
detected a stir in the parlor, and stealing
to the door to listen through the dining-
room, came abruptly upon the old black
woman. Disaster was written on her face
and when she spoke tears came into her
eyes.

" De madam want you," she said, and
passed in to take my place.

As I went on to the parlor, Mrs. Smith,
just inside Mrs. Fontenette's door, beckoned me. As I drew near I made an in-
quiring motion in the direction of our
neighbor across the way.

" I'm hopeful," was her whispered reply;
" but—in here "—she shook her head. Just
then the new maid came from our house,
and Mrs. Smith whispered again—" Go
over quickly to the Baron; he's in his room.
'Twas he came for me. He'll tell you all.
But he'll not tell his wife, and she mustn't
know."

As I ran across the street I divined almost in full what had taken place.

I had noticed the possibility of some of
the facts when I had left the Baron asleep

on the parlor lounge, but they could have
done no harm, even when Senda did not
come, had it not been for two other facts
which I had failed to foresee; one, that we
had unwittingly overtasked our willing old
nurse, and in her chair in Mrs. Fontenette's
room she was going to fall asleep; and the
other that the entomologist would waken.

XXI

AND now see what a cunning trap the
most innocent intentions may sometimes
set. There was a mirror in the sick-room
purposely so placed that, with the parlor
door ajar, the watcher, but not the patient,
could see into the parlor, and could be seen
from the parlor when sitting anywhere between the mirror and the window beyond
it. This window was the one that looked
into the side garden. Purposely, too, the
lounge had been placed so as to give and
receive these advantages. A candle stood
on the window's inner ledge and was
screened from the unseen bed, but shone

The Entomologist

outward through the window and inward
upon the mirror. The front door of the
parlor opened readily to anyone within or
without who knew enough to use its two
latches at once, but neither within nor without to—the Baron, say—who did not know.

Do you see it? As he lay awake on the
lounge his eye was, of course, drawn constantly to the mirror by the reflected light
of the candle, and to its images of the nod-
ding watcher and of the window just beyond. So lying and gazing, he had suddenly beheld that which brought him from
the lounge in an instant, net in hand, and
tortured to find the front door—by which
he would have slipped out and around to
the window—fastened! What he saw was
the moth—the moth so many years unseen.
Now it sipped at the saucer of sweet stuff,
now hovered over it, now was lost in the
dark, and now fluttered up or slid down
the pane, lured by the beam of the candle.

If he was not to lose it, there was but
one thing to do. With his eyes fixed, moth-
mad, on the window, he glided in, passed
the two sleepers, and stealthily lifted the

sash with one hand, the other poising the net. The moth dropped under, the net swept after it, and the sash slipped and fell. Mrs. Fontenette rose wildly, and when she saw first the old woman, half starting from her seat with frightened stare, and then the entomologist speechless, motionless, and looming like an apparition, she gave that cry her husband heard, and fell back upon the pillow in a convulsion.

I found the Baron sitting on the side of his bed like a child trying to be awake without waking. No, not *trying* to do or be anything; but aimless, dazed, silent, lost.

He obeyed, automatically, my every request. I set about getting him to bed at once, putting his clothes beyond his reach, and even locking his balcony door, without a sign of objection from him. Then I left him for a moment, and calling Senda from the nursery to the parlor told her the state of the different patients, including her husband, but without the hows and whys except that I had found him in our garden with his precious net. " And now, as it will soon be day, Mrs. Smith and I—with the servants and others—can take care of the four."

"If I"—meekly interrupted the sweet woman—"vill go for se doctors? I vill go." Soon she was off.

Then I went back to her husband, and finding his mood so changed that he was eager to explain everything, I let him talk; which I soon saw was a blunder; for he got pitifully excited, and wanted to go over the same ground again and again. One matter I was resolved to fix in his mind without delay. "Mark you," I charged him, "your wife must never know a word of this!"

"Eh?—No"—and the next instant the sick woman across the way was filling all his thought: "Mine Gott! she rice oop scaredt in t'e bedt, choost so!" and up he would start. Then as I pressed him down —"Mine Gott! I vould not go in, if I dhink she would do dot. Hmm! Hmm! I am sorry!—Undt I tidt not t'e mawdt get.

"Hmm! Even I titn't saw vhere it iss gone. Hmm! Hmm! I am sorry!

"Undt dot door kit shtuck! Hmm!

Undt dot vindow iss not right made. Hmm!

" I tidn't vant to do dot—you know? Hmm! I am sorry!—Ach, mine Gott! she rice oop scaredt in t'e bedt, choost so! " Thus round and round. What to do for him I did not know!

Yet he grew quiet, and was as good as silent, when Senda, long before I began to look for her, stood unbonneted at my side in a soft glow of physical animation, her anxiety all hidden and with a pink spot on each cheek. I was startled. Had *I* slept —or had she somehow ridden?

" Are the street-cars running already? " I asked.

" No," she murmured, producing a vial and looking for a glass. " 'Tis I haf been running alreadty. Sat iss not so tiresome as to valk. Also it is safeh. I runned all se vay. Vill you sose drops drop faw me? " Her hand trembled.

I took the vial but did not meet her glance: for I was wondering if there was anything in the world she could ask of me that I would not do, and at such a time it is

good for anyone as weak as I am to look
at inanimate things.

"You got word to all three doctors?"

"Yes;" she gave her chin the drollest
little twist—"sey are all coming—vhen sey
get ready."

XXII

THAT is what they did; but the first who
came, and the second, brought fresh courage; for the Baron—"would most likely be
all right again, before the day was over";
our child was "virtually well"; and from
next door—"better!" was the rapturous
news. The third physician, too, was pleased
with Fontenette's case, and we began at
once to send the night-watchers to their rest
by turns.

But there the gladness ended. At Mrs.
Fontenette's bedside he asked no questions.
In the parlor he said to us:

"Well, . . . you've done your best;
. . . I've done mine; . . . and it's
of no use."

"Oh, Doctor!" exclaimed Mrs. Smith.

"Why, didn't you know it?" He jerked his thumb toward the sick-room. "She knows it. She told me she knew it, with her first glance."

He pondered. "I wish she were not so near *him*. If she were only in here—you see?"

Yes, we saw; the two patients would then be, on their either hand, one whole room apart, as if in two squares of a checker-board that touch only at one corner.

"Well," he said, "we must move her at once. I'll show you how; I'll stay and help you."

It seemed more as though we helped him —a very little—as we first moved her and then took the light bedstead apart, set it up again in the parlor, and laid her in it, all without a noticeable sound, and with only great comfort of mind to her—for she knew why we did it. Then I made all haste to my own house again and had the relief to see, as Senda came toward me from her husband's room, that he had told her nothing. "Vell?" she eagerly asked.

196

The Entomologist

"Well, Monsieur Fontenette is greatly improved!"

"O sat iss goodt! And se Madame; she, too, is betteh?—a little?—eh—no-o?"

I said that what the doctor had feared, a "lesion," had taken place, and that there was no longer any hope of her life. At which she lighted up with a lovely defiance.

"Ho-o! no long-eh any hope! Yes, sare *iss* long-er any hope! Vhere iss sat doctoh? Sare *shall* be hope! Kif *me* sat patient! I can keep se vatch of mine hussbandt at se *same* time. *He* hass not a relapse! Kif me se patient! Many ossehs befo'e I haf savedt vhen hadt sose doctohs no long-eh any hope! Mine Gott! vas sare so much hope vhen she and her hussbandt mine sick hussbandt and me out of se street took in? Vill you let stay by mine hussbandt, anyhow a short vhile, one of yo' so goodt sairvants?" The instant I assented she flew down the veranda steps, through the garden, and out across the street.

I lingered a few moments with the entomologist before leaving him with others.

He asked me only one question: " Hmm!
Hmm! How she iss? "

" Why," said I, brightly, " I think she
feels rather more comfortable than she
did."

" Hmm!—Hmm!—I am sorry—Hmm!
—Ach! mine Gott, I am so hoongary!—
Hmm! I am so dtired mit dot sou-oup undt
dose creckers!—Hmm! I vish I haf vonce
a whole pifshtea-ak undt a glahss beer—
hmm! "

" Hmm! " I echoed, " your subsequent
marketing wouldn't cost much." I went
down town on some imperative office business, came back in a cab, gave word to be
called at such an hour, and lay down. But
while I slept my order was countermanded
and when I awakened it was once more
midnight. I went to my open window and
heard, through his balcony door—locked,
now, and its key in my pocket—the Baron,
snoring. Then I sprang into my clothes
and sped across the street.

I went first around to the outer door of
the dining-room, and was briefly told the
best I could have hoped, of Fontenette. I

returned to the front and stepped softly into what had been Mrs. Fontenette's room. Finding no one in it I waited, and when I presently heard voices in the other room, I touched its door-knob. Mrs. Smith came out, closed the door carefully, and sank into a seat.

"It's been a noble fight!" she said, smiling up through her tears. "When the doctor came back and saw how wonderfully the—the worst—had been held off, he joined in the battle! He's been here three times since!"

"And can it be that she is going to pull through?"

My wife's face went down into her hands. "O, no—no. She's dying now—dying in Senda's arms!"

Her ear, quicker than mine, heard some sign within and she left me. But she was back almost at once, whispering:

"She knows you're here, and says she has a message to her husband which she can give only to you."

We gazed into each other's eyes. "Go in," she said.

Strong Hearts

As I entered, Senda tenderly disengaged herself, went out, and closed the door.

I drew near in silence and she began at once to speak, bidding me take the chair Senda had left, and with a tender smile thanking me for coming.

Then she said faintly and slowly, but with an unfaltering voice, " I want you to know one or two things so that if it ever should be my husband's affliction to find out how foolish and undutiful I have been, you can tell them to him. Tell him my wrong-doing was, from first to last, almost totally —almost totally——"

" Do you mean—intangible? "

" Yes, yes, intangible. Then if he should say that the intangible part is the priceless part—the life, the beauty, the very essence of the whole matter—isn't it strange that we women are slower than men to see that— tell him I saw it, saw it and confessed it when for his sake I was slipping away from him by stealth out of life up to my merciful Judge.

" I may not be saying these things in their right order, but—tell him I wish he'd marry again; only let him first be sure the woman loves him as truly and deeply as he is sure to love her. I find I've never truly loved him till now. If he doesn't know it don't ever tell him; but tell him I died loving him and blessing him—for the unearned glorious love he gave me all my days. That's all. That's all to him. But I would like to send one word to "—she lifted her hand——

"Across the street?" I murmured.

Her eyes said yes. "Tell *him*—you may never see the right time for it, but if you do—tell him I craved his forgiveness."

I shook my head.

"Yes—yes, tell him so; it was far the most my fault; he is such a child; such a child of nature, I mean. Tell him I said it sounds very pretty to call ourselves and each other children of nature, but we have no right to be such. The word is ' Be thou clean,' and if we are not masters of nature we can't do it. Tell him that, will you? And tell him he has nothing to grieve for; I was only a dangerous toy, and I want him to love the dear Father for taking it away from him before he had hurt himself.

"Now I am ready to go—only—that hymn those black women—in the cemetery —you remember? I've made another verse to it. You'll find it—afterward—on a scrap of paper between the leaves of my Bible. It isn't good poetry, of course; it's the only verse I ever composed. May I say it to you just for my—my testimony? It's this:

Yet though I have sinned, Lord, all others above,
Though feeble my prayers, Lord; my tears all un-
    seen;
I'll trust in thy love, Lord; I'll trust in thy love—
O I'll trust in thy love like Mary Mahgaleen.

An exalted smile lighted her face as she sunk deeper into the pillows. She tried to speak again, but her voice failed. I bent my ear and she whispered—"Senda."

As I beckoned Senda in, Mrs. Smith motioned for me to come to her where she stood at a window whose sash she had slightly lifted; the same to which the moth had once been lured by the little puddle of sweet drink and the candle.

The Entomologist

" Do you want to see a parable? " she whispered, and all but blinded with tears, she pointed to the lost moth lying half in, half out of the window, still beautiful but crushed; crushed with its wings full spread, not by anyone's choice, but because there are so many things in this universe that not even God can help from being as they are.

At a whispered call we turned, and Senda, in the door, herself all tears, made eager signs for us to come. The last summons had surprised even the dying. We went in noiseless haste, and found her just relaxing on Senda's arm. Yet she revived an instant; a quiver went through her frame like the dying shudder of a butterfly, her eyes gazed appealingly into Senda's, then fixed, and our poor little Titania was gone.

XXIII

THE story is nearly told. Before I close let me confess how heartlessly I have told it. Pardon that; and pardon, too, the self-consciousness that makes me beg not to be remembered as I seem to myself in the tale—a tiptoeing, peeping figure prowling by night after undue revelations, and using them—to the humiliation of souls cleaner than mine could ever pretend to be.

Next day, by stealth again, we buried the little rose-lady, unknown to her husband. We could not keep the fact long from the entomologist, for he was up and about the house again. Nor was there equal need. So when the last rites were over I told him, but without giving any part of her message —I couldn't do it! I just said she had left us.

His eye did not moisten, but he paled, trembled, wiped his brow. Then I handed him the crushed moth, and he was his convalescent self again.

The Entomologist

" Hmm!—Dot iss a pity she kit smashed; I titn't vant to do dot."

I thought maybe he felt more than he showed, for he fretted to be allowed to take a walk alone beyond the gate and the corner. With some misgivings his wife let him go, and when she was almost anxious enough over his tardy stay to start after him he came back looking very much better. But the next morning, when we found him in the burning fever of an unmistakable relapse, he confessed that the German keeper of an eating-stall in the neighboring market, for his hunger's and the Fatherland's sake, had treated him to his " whole pifshtea-ak undt glahss be-eh."

He lived only a few days. Through all his deliriums he hunted butterflies and beetles, and died insensible to his wife's endearments, repeating the Latin conjugations of his inconceivable boyhood.

So they both, caterpillar and rose, were gone; but the memory of them stays, green —yes, and fragrant—not alone with Fontenette, and not only with Senda besides, but with us also. How often I recall the talks on theology I had used sometimes to let myself fall into with the little unsuccessful mistress of " rose-es " who first brought the miser of knowledge into our garden, and whenever I do so I wonder, and wonder, and lose my bearings and find and lose them again, and wonder and wonder —what God has done with the entomologist.

We never had to tell Fontenette that he was widowed. We had only to be long enough silent, and when he ceased, for a time, to get better, and rather lost the strength he had been gaining, and on entering his room we found him always with his face to the wall, we saw that he knew. So for his sake I was glad when one day, without facing round to me, his hand tightened on mine in a wild tremor and he groaned, " Tell it me—tell it."

I told it. I thought it well to give him one of her messages and withhold the rest, like the unscrupulous friend I always try to be; and when he had heard quite through —" Tell him I died loving him and blessing him for the unearned glorious love he gave

me all our days "—he made as if to say the
word was beyond all his deserving, turned
upon his face, and soaked the pillow with
his tears. But from that day he began
slowly but steadily to get well.

We kept Senda with us as long as we
could, and when at length she put her foot
down so that you might have heard it—
say like the dropping of a nut in the wood—
and declared that go she must-must-must!
we first laughed, then scoffed, and then
grew violent, and the battle forced her backward. But when we tried to salary her to
stay, *she* laughed, scoffed, grew violent, and
retook her entrenchments. And then, when
she offered the ultimatum that we must
take pay for keeping her, we took our turn
again at the three forms of demonstration,
and a late moon rose upon a drawn battle.
Since then we have learned to count it one
of our dearest rights to get " put out " at
Senda's outrageous reasonableness, but she
doesn't fret, for " sare is neveh any sundeh
viss se lightening."

The issue of this first contest was decided
the next day by Fontenette, still on his bed

of convalescence. "Can I raise enough money in yo' office to go at France?"

"You can raise twice enough, Fontenette, if it's to try to bring back some new business."

"Well—yes, 'tis for that. Of co'se, besides——"

"Yes, I know: of course."

"But tha'z what puzzle' me. What I'm going do with that house heah, whilse I'm yondeh! I wou'n' sell it—ah, no! I wou'n' sell one of those roses! An' no mo' I wou'n' rent it. Tha's a monument, that house heah, you know?"

"Yes, I know." He never found out how well I knew.

"Fontenette, I'll tell you what to do with it."

"No, you don't need; I know whad thad is. An' thaz the same I want—me. Only —you thing thad wou'n' be hasking her too much troub'?"

"No, indeed. There's nothing else you could name that she'd be so glad to do."

When I told Senda I had said that, the tears stood in her eyes. "Ah, sat vass

ri-ight! O, sare shall neveh a veed be in
sat karten two dayss oldt! An' sose roses
—sey shall be pairfect ever' vun!"

XXIV

As perfect as roses every one were her
words kept. And Fontenette got his new
business but could not come back that year,
nor the second, nor the third. The hither-
side of his affairs he assigned for the time
to a relative, a very young fellow, but ever
so capable—"a hustler," as our fat friend
would say in these days. We missed the
absentee constantly, but forgave his deten-
tion the easier because incidentally he was
clearing up a matter of Senda's over there,
in which certain displeased kindred had
overreached her. Also because of his letters
to her, which she so often did us the honor
to show us.

The first few were brief, formal and color-
less; but after some time they began to take
on grace after grace, until at length we had
to confess that to have known him only as

we had known him hitherto would have been to have been satisfied with the reverse of the tapestry, and never fully to have seen the excellence of his mind or the modest nobility of his spirit. Frequently we felt very sure we saw also that no small share of their captivating glow was reflected from Senda's replies—of which she never would tell us a word. The faults in his written English were surprisingly few, and to our minds only the more endeared it and him. Maybe we were not judicial critics.

Yet we could pass strictures, and as the months lengthened out into years these winged proxies stirred up, on our side of the street, a profound and ever-growing impatience. O, yes, every letter was a garden of beautiful thoughts, still; but think of it! *pansies* where roses might have been; and a garden wherein—to speak figuratively—the nightingale never sang.

On a certain day of All Saints, the fourth after the scourge, Senda sat at tea with us. Our mood was chastened, but peaceful. We had come from visiting at the sunset hour the cemetery where in the morning the two

women and our old nurse had decked the
tombs of our dead with flowers. I had
noticed that at no tomb front were these
tokens piled more abundantly, or more
beautifully or fragrantly, than at those of
Flora and the entomologist; it was always
so. I had remarked this on the spot, and
Senda, with her rearranging touch still
caressing their splendid masses, replied,

"So?—Vell—I hope siss shall mine vork
and mine pleassure be until mineself I shall
fade like se floweh."

I inwardly resented the speech, but said
nothing. I suppose it was over my head.

Now, at the table, she explained as to
certain costly blooms about which I had inquired, that they were Fontenctte's special
offering, for which he always sent the purchase money ahead of time and with detailed requests. Whereat, remembering
how she had formerly glozed and gilded
the entomologist's unthrift, I remarked,
one-fourth in play, three-fourths in earnest,

"A good plain business man isn't the
least noble work of God, after all."

"No," said Senda, without looking up;

and, after a long, meditative breath, she added, very slowly,

"Se koot Kott makes not all men for se same high calling. If Kott make a man to do no betteh san make a living or a fawtune, it iss right for se man to make it; se *man* iss not to blame. And now I vant to tell you se news of sat letteh from——"

"The other side," we suggested, and invited her smile, but without success.

"Yes, from se osseh si-ide; sat letteh vhat you haf brought me since more as a veek *a*go; and also vhy I haf not sat letteh given you to read. Sat iss—if you like to know —yes?

"Vell, sen I vill tell you. And sare are two sings to tell. Se fairst is a ve'y small, but se secondt iss a ve'y lahge. And se fairst is sat that *I* am now se Countess.

"So? you are glad? I sank you ve'y much. I sink sat iss not much trouble—to be a countess—in Ame'ica?

"Se secondt sing"—'here a servant entered, and, it seemed to me, never would go out, but Senda waited till we were again alone—"se secondt—pahdon me, I sink I shall betteh se secondt sing divide again into two aw sree. And se fairst is sat Monsieur Fontenette vill like ve'y—ve'y much to come home—now—right avay."

We lifted hands to clap and opened mouths to hurrah, but she raised a warning hand.

" No, vait—if you pleass.

" Se secondt of sose two or sree sings—it is sat—he—Monsieur Fontenette—hass ask me—" Our hearts rose slowly into our throats—" Ze vun qvestion to vich sare can be only—se—vun—answeh."

At this we gulped our breath like schoolgirls and glowed. But the more show we made of hopeful and pleading smiles, the more those dear eyes, so seldom wet, filled up with tears.

" *He* sinks sare can two answehs be, and he like to heah which is se answeh I shall gif him, so he shall know if he shall come—now—aw if he shall come—neveh.

" O my sweet friend,"—to Mrs. Smith, down whose face the salt drops stole unhindered—" sare iss nossing faw *you* to cry." She smiled heroically.

I could be silent no longer. "Senda, what have you answered?"

"I haf answered"—her lips quivered till she gnawed them cruelly—"I am sorry to take such a long time to tell you sat—but —I—I find sat—ve'y hahd—to tell." She smiled and gnawed her lips again. "I haf answered—

"Do you sink, my deah, sat siss is ri-ight to tell the ve'y vords sat I haf toldt him?— yes?—vell—he tell me I shall se answeh make in vun vord—is sat not like a man?

"But I had to take six. And sey are sese: I cannot vhispeh across se ocean."